Goodbye,

Amanda

the

Good

Goodbye, Amanda the Good

SUSAN SHREVE

Alfred A. Knopf
New York

THIS IS A BORZOI BOOK PUBLISHED BY ALFRED A. KNOPF, INC.

Copyright © 2000 by Susan Shreve
Jacket illustration copyright © 2000 by Tristan Elwell

All rights reserved under International and Pan-American Copyright
Conventions. Published in the United States of America by Alfred A. Knopf,
a division of Random House, Inc., New York, and simultaneously in Canada
by Random House of Canada Limited, Toronto.
Distributed by Random House, Inc., New York.
KNOPF, BORZOI BOOKS, and the colophon are registered trademarks
of Random House, Inc.

www.randomhouse.com/kids

Library of Congress Cataloging-in-Publication Data
Shreve, Susan Richards.
Goodbye, Amanda the good / by Susan Shreve.
p.   cm.
Summary: After three months as a nobody in junior high, Amanda finds her
world changing when members of the popular and exclusive clique The Club
set their sights on her for membership.
ISBN 0-679-89241-9 (trade) — ISBN 0-679-99241-3 (lib. bdg.)
[1. Popularity—Fiction. 2. Clubs—Fiction. 3. Schools—Fiction.] I. Title.
√ Curr PZ7.S55915 Gp 2000
[Fic]—dc21   99-045408
Printed in the United States of America
March 2000
First Edition
10 9 8 7 6 5 4 3 2 1

To Hannah,

of course

CHAPTER ONE

Amanda Bates stood at the bathroom sink on the Monday after Thanksgiving, looking in the mirror at her hair, which was the color of purple grapes. On the floor were two of her mother's yellow terry cloth bath towels, now striped purple, and a box of hair dye labeled INK with a picture on it of a woman whose long, shiny hair was black. *Not* purple.

Ink was the color Fern had dyed her hair two days before Thanksgiving. Fern was the most powerful member of the Club at Alice Deal Junior High, where Amanda was in the seventh grade. She and Amanda were not friends. In fact, until that morning in the girls' room, after social studies class, Fern had never even spoken to Amanda. But that day, while Amanda was washing her hands, glancing in the mirror to check her own hair, Fern had said, "Hi" and asked if Amanda had a spare cigarette.

"Not right now," Amanda had replied, although she had never smoked a cigarette in her life. But it was exactly the right answer to give Fern, suggesting that at some other time she might have a cigarette.

"I like your hair color," Amanda added, hoping to initiate a friendship, since there was no girl in all of Alice Deal Junior High that she would have liked to have as a friend more than Fern, formerly Barbara Adams, president of the Club.

"Thanks." Fern examined herself in the mirror. "Ink is the name on the hair dye box."

Now it was late afternoon, and Amanda's house was empty except for her younger brother, Joshua, who had just been promoted to the fourth grade in the middle of the year, after flunking third grade.

When Amanda walked without knocking into his bedroom, he was lying faceup on his bed with Plutarch, the family cat, unhappily locked under his arm. Joshua's eyes widened.

"Don't say anything," she said. "I know already. It's a disaster." She reached up and touched her purple bangs. "I dyed it, in case you wondered." She sat down on the end of Joshua's bed. "It was supposed to turn out black."

"I think you better do something about it before Mom gets home from the grocery store with Georgie," Joshua said, making a face. "It looks pretty disgusting."

"Like *what* should I do?" She checked herself in the full-length mirror on Joshua's closet door. "Shave it?"

"Like dye it back to your own color."

"Brown is boring. That's why I dyed it in the first place," Amanda said.

"Then dye it a normal color like blond."

"Maybe Sable. They had a color called Sable in the hair products department at CVS."

"So let's go to CVS, pronto," Joshua said, putting on his coat. Amanda wrote

```
Getting school supplies,
            A and J
```

on the blackboard in the kitchen underneath her mother's message:

```
At the grocery store with
Georgianna. Back at six.
            Love, M
```

She put on her ski jacket, pulled up the hood to cover her purple hair, and followed Joshua out the back door.

"I hate Alice Deal," Amanda said as they headed up Lowell Street in the dark. "If you're not in a group, it's miserable."

"I know," Joshua said sadly. "My first day in the fourth grade was miserable."

"But at least you have friends," Amanda said. "I have none. Zero. Everyone in the whole seventh grade belongs to some group or another."

The only group Amanda could imagine joining was the Club, even though she was sure they were not about to invite her. The Club was the fringe group at Alice Deal. They were known for their loyalty to one another and their contempt for authority figures, particularly teachers and parents and police. They were recognized by their manner of dress—tattoos, real ones that didn't wash off in the shower, and pierced ears or noses or lips or belly buttons. Amanda had seen the silver stud in Fern's belly button when they were dressing after phys ed. They dyed their hair and wore tight, tight skirts and tiny tops that left a strip of bare skin showing just above their waists, and clunky shoes. They smoked cigarettes and had a way of talking in whispers, which gave the impression they were telling secrets, excluding everyone who wasn't a member of their group.

Amanda admired their nerve. She liked that they changed their names, as Fern had done, going from Barbara Adams to just Fern. They were brave and daring and rebellious, afraid of nothing, and Amanda Bates, who had been a good, obedient girl for all her life, wanted to be one of them.

There were other groups at Alice Deal—the athletes,

who included the sports teams as well as the ninth-grade cheerleaders and the gymnasts and the Montgomery County Soccer Team. There were the regulars—called that with disdain by members of the Club—who were well liked and good students, and who followed the rules of the school—the group to which Amanda would have belonged in elementary school. There were the visual artists, dancers and drama students, and members of the school chorus, who filled their free time with lessons and rehearsals.

But the Club was different. Membership was by invitation and not by luck, with rules for joining and standards of behavior and a common demeanor, as if all of the members were from the same family, imitating one another's gestures and dress and way of speaking. Amanda believed the Club's opinions were valued and feared and admired by all the seventh-grade girls. Deep down, she herself was dying to be a member.

Just months ago, Amanda had been living an ordinary, easy, predictable life. She'd get up in the morning, put on her jeans, a T-shirt, and a sweater, and go downstairs for breakfast with her parents, who glowed with pleasure in her company. She'd walk to Mirch Elementary, sometimes with Joshua, sometimes with her friends, and spend the day getting A's and "Excellent"s and commendations in all of her classes, invitations to everybody's birthday party. She even had a boyfriend, Bruce Griffith, a little nerdy according to Joshua, but almost as smart as Amanda. They talked at lunchtime and walked home together, since he lived a few blocks beyond Lowell Street. For graduation from sixth grade, he gave her an unopened bottle of CK1 cologne and a note on stationery that had a sailing ship at the top:

Thank you for being the best
girlfriend I ever had.
            Your friend,
      Bruce Griffith

Her days had been simple. She did her homework quickly after dinner, went to bed, fell immediately asleep, and woke up cheerful in the morning. "Mary Sunshine," her father sometimes called her.

And then, the summer before the beginning of seventh grade, on a specific day, a Tuesday in early August, she happened to catch a glimpse of herself in her mother's full-length mirror. And she stopped short, looking at a reflection she did not know. There she stood in her khaki shorts, hard to pull up over her bottom and a little tight at the belly, and white T-shirt, her hair in a high ponytail with a lavender scrunchie, and she looked entirely different from the way she had looked the day before. It was as if she were looking at herself in a fun-house mirror that distorted her reflection. She looked rectangular instead of square. Her face was oddly shaped, longer than it had been before she went to bed, sharper, older, as if the child she had been had slipped away during the night, replaced by this other, unappealing girl reflected in the mirror in her mother's room.

She went downstairs for breakfast in a bad mood. When her mother asked what the trouble was, she said, "None of your business." When her father said he'd have "no adolescent posturing" in his house, she raised her eyebrows, assumed an expression of absolute boredom, and said in that case she'd be happy to move out of his house.

That day, the summer divided in two parts. On the one side of summer was the life Amanda Bates had lived since she was born. On the other was this different life. She was no longer at ease or settled in, or familiar with her own body. She was at war with the world, narrowing her eyes at her parents when she sat down to dinner, locking the door to her bedroom, playing her radio at top volume. She was vaguely unhappy all the time, with a constant feeling of dread in the pit of her stomach.

She felt as if she had taken a leap off the high diving board into the lake in New Hampshire where the Bateses went for summer vacation. But the water kept moving farther and farther away from her as she flew—arms flailing, legs kicking out of control—downward through the cold air.

In the fall of seventh grade, when Amanda started Alice Deal and assessed where she might fit in, who would be her friends, how she would make a life for herself in junior high school, she was worried. None of her four good friends from Mirch Elementary were going to Alice Deal. Sally had moved to Israel, and Rachel was going to private school and the twins to Whitman High, in Bethesda. Bruce Griffith was at Alice Deal, but he wore his pants too high on his waist and his hair long and frizzy, and his eyes were forlorn behind black-rimmed glasses—the eyes of a basset hound. Amanda avoided him in the corridors, embarrassed to be friends with a straight-A student who looked like a nerd. The other kids who had known Amanda from Mirch Elementary thought of her as smart, a teacher's pet, always at the top of the class, recognized for good citizenship, too perfect to be true. It was not, Amanda decided, a good reputation to have in junior high school.

At CVS, Amanda bought two boxes of Sable hair dye, in case one didn't cover the purple, and a copy of *True Teen*, which had an article on hair.

"Which do you like?" she asked Joshua, showing him a picture of six different hairstyles. They were standing in the checkout line.

Joshua looked at the picture and shook his head. "They all look sick," he said.

"I'm thinking of wearing my hair in a spiky ponytail," Amanda said, paying for her magazine and hair dye. "Sort of sassy."

"Why are you doing all this stuff?" Joshua asked.

"I'm bored with always looking the same as I did yesterday, but I don't know," Amanda said truthfully. "Fern, the girl I told you about, spoke to me today in the girls' room."

"So maybe she wants to be friends," Joshua said.

"Maybe."

By the time Mrs. Bates got back from the store with Georgie and was in the kitchen making pasta and tomato sauce for dinner, and Mr. Bates was standing by the TV, his hands in his pockets, watching the evening news, Amanda's hair was Sable with only a hint of purple.

"Not bad," Joshua said, watching his sister blow-dry her hair. "Not awful, at least."

"Do you like it in this kind of ponytail?"

"It's okay." Joshua shrugged. "Sort of like a fox terrier's tail."

Amanda shook her hair like a mop, pleased with herself.

"I love fox terriers," she said. "They're my number-one favorite dog."

▲　○　■

No one brought up Amanda's hair at first, although her mother raised her eyebrows and exchanged a look with her father. Her parents were mainly interested in hearing about Joshua's first day in the fourth grade. They wanted to know how he had liked it and what had happened in every class and if the boys, especially the ones who had been unkind when he flunked third grade, had been nice to him.

Joshua said his first day was great, which Amanda happened to know was not the truth, and finally they turned their attention to Amanda.

"So what's up with you?" Mr. Bates asked Amanda, pretending he hadn't seen the color of her hair.

"Not much," Amanda said, practicing her new skill in short responses.

"How's school?" Mrs. Bates asked.

"A disaster," Amanda said.

"Shouldn't your report card be here by now?" Mr. Bates asked. "We got Joshua's before Thanksgiving."

"It'll be here soon, I suppose," Amanda said.

Her parents looked up from their dinners.

"It won't be all A's," she added. "In case that's what you're expecting."

"We're not expecting all A's, darling," her mother said.

"There may be very few A's," Amanda said, knowing that the only A she could possibly receive was in physical education. The rest of her grades would be C's unless she got a B in English, and maybe even a D in math.

"Junior high is different," her mother said. "It's an adjustment, and I'm sure as soon as you feel comfortable, you'll be back on top of the academics."

Amanda didn't reply. She could feel her father staring at her. He reached over and tugged her ponytail.

"A fashion statement?" he asked.

"I don't know what you're talking about," Amanda said, giving him a level look. "I just put my hair up."

"And dyed it," Mrs. Bates said sadly.

"Sable," Amanda said evenly. "That's the name on the box."

After dinner, Amanda went upstairs to her room, dragging her book bag with her homework in math and language arts, which she had no plans to do, and turned on the light in her bedroom. Spread out on her bed were the two yellow towels striped with purple dye, which she had left on the bathroom floor. And next to them, written on lined paper with purple Magic Marker, was a note from her mother:

> Please wash the towels
> until they are yellow again.
>
> Your formerly beloved mother

CHAPTER TWO

On Tuesday, Amanda was late to school. She kept sleeping after the alarm went off, and then she had an argument with her mother because she wouldn't eat breakfast.

"Just a banana," Mrs. Bates said.

"I'm not hungry," Amanda insisted, grabbing her book bag and heading toward the door.

Mrs. Bates followed her, thrusting a banana and a carton of yogurt at her, talking about potassium and blood sugar levels.

"I'm not hungry," Amanda said through her teeth. She was just about to leave for school when her father came in, holding her report card.

"Where was it?" Mrs. Bates asked.

"The mailman came this morning," Mr. Bates said in a

tone of voice that indicated he had already seen the bad news.

"I'm late for school," Amanda said. "We can talk at dinner."

But Mr. Bates didn't want to talk at dinner. "I'll drive you to school and we'll talk now," he said.

So Amanda climbed reluctantly into the front seat of the Ford van, which smelled of cat pee from taking Plutarch to the vet's, and faced straight ahead.

"This report card is disturbing," Mr. Bates said, his voice strangely calm, as if at any moment he might erupt in a volcanic rage, as he sometimes did. He took the report card out of his pocket and put it in her lap. All C's except for a B in phys. ed, and D's in math and social studies.

"Disturbing?" Amanda asked, as if she had no clue what he could be referring to.

"You've always been a straight-A student, Amanda," her father said, his hands tight on the steering wheel. "It's disturbing when a person changes her behavior."

"Things change." She turned to face the street, watching the sidewalk and the groups of seventh graders hurrying across Nebraska Avenue.

"Not this much," Mr. Bates said. "These are C's and D's."

"School is harder in seventh grade," Amanda said. "We

have a different teacher for every subject. They don't get to know the students. The kids who are noisy and talk out of turn do the best."

"It's not like you to blame other kids for your problems," Mr. Bates said, pulling to a stop in front of the school.

"How do you know what's like me and what isn't? I'm a different person than I used to be." Amanda opened the door of the van and hopped out onto the sidewalk. She walked across the lawn and up the steps to the green main door of Alice Deal Junior High without looking back, although her breathing was shallow and she was shaking. In all her years of growing up, she had never talked back to her father. She turned as she opened the door, looking back to where the van had been, planning to wave goodbye or smile or make some kind of gesture of apology. But her father had already gone.

On her way to her locker, Amanda passed the Honor Roll, which was posted outside the principal's office, and out of habit she stopped to glance at it, checking the B's. Not that she had any expectation that her name would be there, or even wished for it to be. But it was the first marking period since third grade that she hadn't been on the Honor Roll, and for a fleeting moment, she felt a sadness.

She didn't even notice Slade Springer until she turned around. He was standing so close behind her she should have been able to feel his breath on the back of her neck.

"So is your name on the Honor Roll?" he asked.

"I doubt it," she said.

"I've never made the Honor Roll in my life," he said, leaning against the wall beside her.

As far as Amanda was concerned, Slade Springer, known only as Slade, was the most handsome boy in the ninth grade, maybe in all of Alice Deal Junior High, with his baggy jeans and black leather jacket and baseball cap set backward on his head, flattening the black curly hair he wore long. He had a reputation for bad behavior, and everyone knew he had a large black crow tattooed on his right forearm. Amanda had never seen him smoke a cigarette at school, but she noticed the shiny red pack peeking out of his jacket pocket, and according to conversations Amanda had overheard in the locker room, he had a lighter with S L A D E engraved on the front, which had been given to him by his last girlfriend, Brianna Baker, who had moved away in October.

"You're Amanda," Slade said, shifting his book bag.

"Yes," she replied, out of breath, her heart racing. "How do you know my name?"

"I've noticed you in the cafeteria lately, and I just asked around." He smiled at her with a funny crooked smile, a deep dimple appearing in his chin. "I'm Slade."

"I know," she said.

Everyone knows, she wanted to add. *Every girl here knows exactly who you are and what you do every minute of the day and what you wear to school and what you have for lunch and who you hang out with after school.*

"You used to go out with Brianna." She couldn't think of anything else to say.

"You know Brianna?"

"No, but I've heard of her," Amanda said.

"Brianna's moved away for good," he said, leaning just close enough to brush against Amanda's arm.

"That's terrible for you," she said, not knowing exactly how to talk to him.

Slade shrugged. "I'll live." He checked the Honor Roll. "What's your last name?"

"Bates," Amanda said.

"No Bates here," he said. "Fern told me you were smart."

Amanda wasn't sure what to say. *Yes, I'm smart,* or *I used to be smart,* or *Would you like me to be smart?* But instead she told him the truth—that she used to be smart and now she wasn't, which made him laugh.

"You know Fern?" she asked.

He rolled his eyes. "Since I was in second grade at Lafayette and she was in kindergarten. She was always sitting in a chair outside the classroom for bad behavior."

"So," Amanda said, hoping to sound flip, "I suppose she was your girlfriend."

"Not exactly. Not Fern," he said, smiling at her. "Hey, why don't you meet me in front of Bread and Chocolate on Wednesday before school?" he asked, following Amanda to her locker. "I go there at about seven-thirty and get some coffee."

"Sure," she said quietly, taking her books out of her locker, trying to pretend this moment with Slade was ordinary. "That'll be great."

He gave her a little box on the shoulder. And then he was gone, around the corner of the library and down the steps to the ninth-grade classrooms.

Fern appeared out of nowhere and followed Amanda into first-period social studies.

"Dyed your hair?" she asked, falling into step as they walked down the corridor past the gym. "I like it."

"Thanks," Amanda said.

"Sable, right?"

Amanda nodded.

"Sit next to me," Fern said, indicating a desk at the back of the room. "Ms. Englander is a dog." She narrowed her eyes at the bone-thin young teacher at the front of the class. "Did I see you talking to Slade?" she asked.

"I was."

"I didn't know you knew him," Fern said, opening her book bag and offering Amanda a piece of gum.

"I don't. We just met. He knew my name."

Fern rolled her eyes. "Right. Just like Slade. He probably asked you out."

"Not out," Amanda said, putting her social studies book on her desk. "He asked me to meet him at Bread and Chocolate before school tomorrow."

"Well, don't get your hopes up," Fern said.

"I don't have any hopes," Amanda said defensively. "When he asked me, I just thought why not?"

"Exactly. I'd do it too if I didn't already have a boyfriend," Fern said, making a face at Ms. Englander, whose back was turned toward them. "Just be careful with Slade. He's a *real* hunk, but he's got a reputation for dropping girls if they don't do anything with him."

"'Do anything'?"

"You know what I mean." Fern gave Amanda a look as if she were stupid beyond belief. "Put out."

"Oh yeah," Amanda said, although she wasn't at all sure what Fern meant by the words "put out." Sex, she imagined. She had read the "don't you dare bring home" magazines at the newsstand, and in the sixth grade she had had conversations about sex with her friends. But she had never done anything herself. She hadn't even dreamed of it.

"Don't worry," Amanda said. "I know all about guys like Slade."

Which wasn't true, of course. Besides Joshua, the only boy she really knew well was her sixth-grade boyfriend, Bruce Griffith.

Ms. Englander asked Amanda to stay after class.

"Trouble?" Fern asked.

"Maybe. I haven't done my social studies project yet."

"Who has? Certainly not me," Fern said.

"I got a D," Amanda said.

"Don't worry. Social studies is a throwaway course."

Amanda gathered her books and started toward the front of the room, where Ms. Englander was waiting.

"See you later," she said to Fern.

"See you on the blacktop after lunch."

"Great," Amanda said, filling with excitement.

Fern was alone, leaning against the building next to the gym entrance when Amanda came out of the lunchroom. It was a bright, cold afternoon, but Fern wasn't wearing a coat, only a sweater, a black beret, and leopard-patterned gloves.

"You're a slow eater," Fern said. "I've been here for hours." She scanned the area. "I was looking for Slade, to give him the cigarettes he left at my house yesterday, but he hasn't come out yet." She pulled a pack of cigarettes from under her sweater. "Want one?" She smiled and stuffed the pack away.

"So Slade comes over a lot?" Amanda asked, hoping to change the subject. She kept her voice casual.

Fern shrugged. "Some," she said. "A few times a week if I'm not busy with Club things." She raised her eyebrows. "Don't think he's my boyfriend."

"I didn't," Amanda said, leaning against the building next to Fern. "It never crossed my mind."

"He's not. I've just known him forever and we're kind of alike. Bad seeds is what my mother calls us."

"Slade told me you've been friends since elementary."

"Sort of like confidants," Fern said. "He tells me pretty much everything."

She waved to two girls coming out of the school, giving them a thumbs-down. "That's Anastasia and Bronco. Usually we go out beyond the soccer field for a smoke after lunch, but today I'm talking to you."

And Fern gave her a large, bright smile, as if she had just decided that Amanda Bates was worth getting to know.

CHAPTER THREE

When the alarm went off at six in the morning on the Wednesday after Thanksgiving, Amanda was lying in bed thinking of changing her name to Cheetah—just Cheetah, dropping the Bates. She turned off the alarm, threw the covers on the floor, and jumped out of bed. She was wide awake. In fact, she had barely slept, although she certainly wasn't going to let her parents know that. Her eyes had been tightly closed when her mother had come in to kiss her good night the night before. She had slipped her alarm under her pillow so they wouldn't hear it go off an hour earlier than usual and suspect something.

She opened the door to her closet. She had planned to wear her short red skirt, her white V-necked sweater, and the clunky black shoes that she'd told her mother *everyone* at Alice Deal Junior High was wearing. She was embarrassed to wear sneakers. No girl wore sneakers in seventh grade. But when she tried on the skirt, Amanda thought the bright red made her hips, which had recently begun to spread, expand to the width of a full-sized van. So she tossed the red skirt on the floor and tried on a little black skirt that had belonged to her cousin.

The black skirt looked better than the red one had. But the white V-necked sweater was terrible. It showed the outline of her newborn nipples even with a bra and slipped off her shoulders like a nightgown, so she threw it on top of the red skirt, pulled down the pile of sweaters from a shelf in her closet, and found a very old one that was a hand-me-down from her mother. It was black and big. When she put it on, she couldn't see her nipples—or her breasts at all—and she was pleased to note that it covered her enormous hips. She slipped on black tights and the clunky black shoes, which made her five feet four inches instead of five feet two; brushed her hair into a high ponytail; and took a stash of makeup, which she kept hidden for obvious reasons, from under the bed.

On the blacktop the day before, Fern had suggested Dark Plum lipstick with matching nail polish, double-thick black mascara, and a deep pinkish blush, high on her cheeks. Amanda thought the makeup gave her a sunken look, as if she were starving.

"It's a very good look for you, especially with Sable hair," Fern had said.

Amanda didn't put on the makeup now. She planned to stop at the ladies' room at the Exxon station on Connecticut Avenue, across the street from Bread and Chocolate, where she was meeting Slade at seven-thirty.

Joshua was brushing his teeth in the bathroom with the door open when Amanda came out of her bedroom to go downstairs. It wasn't even seven o'clock yet.

"What are you doing up so early?" Amanda asked, leaning against the door. She wanted to ask Joshua whether he liked the way she looked, but she wasn't sure she could count on his opinion.

"Your alarm woke me up," Joshua said, putting his toothbrush away and wiping the toothpaste off his mouth with his pajama sleeve. "It woke Georgianna, too."

Georgianna was sitting on the closed toilet seat. "Georgie sick," she said solemnly.

"I don't know how you heard the alarm," Amanda said, ignoring Georgianna. "It was under my pillow."

"Georgie sick," Georgianna said again.

"What's the matter with Georgie?" Amanda asked, checking her hair in the mirror.

Georgianna shook her head sadly.

"She wants attention," Joshua said, picking Georgianna up. "She's starved for attention." He handed her to Amanda.

"Yuck," Amanda said. "You smell bad, Georgie."

"Exactly," Joshua said, going into his own room.

"Where's Mom?" Amanda asked.

"Night-night," Georgie said.

"Wrong. Mom's not 'night-night' any longer," Joshua called from his room. "She's downstairs making breakfast."

"Already?" Amanda carried Georgie into her bedroom to change her diaper.

She had hoped she would be able to leave early, by seven, before anyone was downstairs to ask her questions about the way she looked and why she was leaving so early. She wanted time to walk to the Exxon station and put on the makeup, which she had slipped into the zippered pocket of her book bag, in time to get to Bread and Chocolate by seven-thirty. Slade would be waiting for her there, maybe smoking while he leaned against the building.

"I won't be able to walk with you today," she called to Joshua. "I'm not going the usual way."

"No big deal," Joshua said, appearing at the doorway, his book bag slung over his shoulder. "Where're you going?"

"To meet a friend for breakfast."

"Yeah?" Joshua came into Georgianna's room, where

Amanda had finished changing their baby sister's diaper. "A guy?"

"Kind of."

"What sort of guy?" Joshua leaned over the bed and tickled Georgianna's belly.

"None of your business, Joshua."

"None of the business of me, your brother, who used to know everything?"

"There was nothing to know. All I did in sixth grade was study." Amanda stood Georgie up and put her in her overalls. "I was completely boring."

"Is he your boyfriend?"

"Nope," Amanda said. "He's not my boyfriend." She picked Georgie up. "But you can't tell Mom."

"Cross my heart."

"Or Dad."

"I'm good at secrets."

He followed Amanda as she carried Georgianna downstairs.

At the foot of the stairs, Amanda looked back at her brother. "What do you think of the word 'cheetah'?" she asked him, putting down Georgie, who trotted into the kitchen, where her mother was cooking oatmeal and her father was reading the newspaper and Plutarch was lying on his back, licking his belly.

"It's a nice-enough word," Joshua said.

"I mean really. Do you think it's a good name for someone?"

Joshua looked at her. "For what kind of person?"

"Just a regular person," Amanda said.

"Like you?"

"Sort of."

"I think it's a terrible name for you, if that's what you're asking," Joshua said. "It's not a normal name for a girl."

Amanda shrugged. "I'm getting a little tired of my own name," she said.

"Then why don't you call yourself Sarah or Elizabeth or Kate, something normal?"

"I just don't like normal anymore," Amanda said crossly, irritated that Joshua, on whom she counted for understanding, didn't understand.

"Whose funeral is it today?" Mr. Bates asked, putting down his newspaper as Amanda walked into the kitchen.

"If you're talking to me, I don't know what you're talking about," Amanda said, sitting down in the chair next to her father and pouring cereal into her bowl—just a small amount, less than half a bowl, because she was thinking of the size of her hips.

"You'll starve before lunch," her mother said, trying to comfort Georgianna.

"I won't starve. People without any food starve," she said.

"That's not necessarily true," her father said. "There are people here in Washington who don't have enough to eat, and other people who do have enough and refuse to eat it."

"I'm not trying to have a political debate," Amanda said. "I'm trying to eat my cereal *quietly*."

"A good idea," Mr. Bates said. "I absolutely hate to listen to you when you eat your cereal *noisily*."

Amanda ignored him.

Her parents were driving her crazy. For years she had loved them, loved everything about them, filling with warmth whenever she saw them. Now they annoyed her when they spoke in their know-it-all voices, and they embarrassed her, even at the supermarket, crowded with strangers.

"So tell me, who has died?" her father asked.

"I suppose you're making fun of what I have on," Amanda said sarcastically.

"Not at all," her father said, putting the newspaper on the floor and pouring himself more coffee. "I'm *interested* in what you have on. It's a very black outfit."

"I like black," Amanda said, not finishing her cereal, too excited to eat. She packed her book bag, zipped it, and put it over her shoulder. "I've always liked black."

"Where are you going so early?" her mother asked. "It's only ten of seven."

"I have an appointment," Amanda said.

"At school?" her father asked.

"With my social studies teacher," Amanda said, lying easily.

"Raincoat?" her mother asked, standing by the back door, where she usually stood to kiss her children goodbye on their way to school.

"I don't need one," Amanda said, irritated at her mother for invading her life with clothing suggestions, always irritated lately.

"It's supposed to rain, darling," her mother said, leaning down to kiss the top of Amanda's head.

"Then I guess I'll get wet."

And Amanda walked out the back door, down the steps, through the back gate, and down the path to Lowell Street, without once looking back to wave.

CHAPTER FOUR

Slade wasn't there.

Amanda had arrived early. She leaned against the window outside Bread and Chocolate, just so, one leg crossed over the other, her Dark Plum lips pouty, like the lips of models in *Seventeen.*

She had gotten to the Exxon station at seven-fifteen, which gave her plenty of time to put on the makeup in her book bag. The lipstick was easy. She made her lips just a little larger than they were, pushing them out and kissing herself in the bathroom mirror of the filling station. The mascara was difficult. It globbed on her eyelashes like peanut butter. When she tried to wipe it off with toilet paper, it got all over her eyelids, and when she finally got it on right—on her lashes and not her eyelids—her eyes were bloodshot from the irritation.

▲   ○   ■

The manager of Bread and Chocolate came outside and asked her not to lean against the glass.

"I'm meeting someone," Amanda said.

"Wait inside," the woman said.

"But maybe he won't be able to find me."

"I don't care where you wait, miss, just don't lean against the glass. Got it?"

"Right," Amanda said. Just a few months ago, she would have apologized. Trembling, she would have said how sorry she was and moved away from the glass and worried that the manager might call her mother. Then again, a few months ago she'd never have dared to come here by herself. But now she lowered her eyes and said, "Right," and moved a fraction of an inch away from the glass.

By seven-forty-five, Slade still had not arrived. Amanda couldn't hold the pout on her face any longer, and she was weary of standing, so she paced in front of the restaurant, looking up and down the street, hoping to catch a glimpse of him.

Maybe something had happened, she thought. Maybe he'd gotten into an accident, or the subway was stuck between stations, or he'd woken up with pneumonia and didn't have her telephone number to let her know he wouldn't be there.

"Miss," the manager said, coming out again. "You're bothering my customers, walking back and forth in front of the window. I wonder if you'd either come inside or leave."

Amanda checked her watch against the clock across the street. Both said eight-ten.

"Maybe your friend has forgotten," the manager said.

"I'm sure he hasn't," Amanda said in her coldest voice, looking north toward Alice Deal. "He's probably sick."

"Whatever." The manager turned away and walked back inside.

It was after eight-thirty when Amanda arrived at Alice Deal, a little breathless, her lipstick faded, a dark line of charcoal mascara rubbed across her cheek.

"I'm late," she said to the secretary at the principal's office.

"Evidently," the secretary said. "Second day in a row." She pushed a clipboard with the late sign-in sheet in front of Amanda, who signed her name in her new scrawly handwriting with a small "a" for Amanda and a small "b" for Bates. "Did you bring an excuse?"

"I had a dentist's appointment," Amanda said, turning to leave.

The secretary looked at the sign-in sheet. "Amanda Bates?"

"Yes."

"I believe your mother just called the office to say she's picking you up at one-thirty for a dentist's appointment. Two in one day?" the secretary asked.

"I have bad teeth."

"What class do you have second period?"

"Math," Amanda said.

"Well, go straight there."

Instead, Amanda stopped at the telephone and dialed the office where Mrs. Bates was a part-time lawyer, having worked only in the mornings since Georgianna had been born.

"I'm *not* going to the dentist," she said when her mother picked up.

"You have to go, Amanda," her mother said. "They were able to take you today because someone else canceled."

"They'll have to find someone else to fit in," Amanda said, and hung up.

She put her jacket in her locker, took out her math book; a copy of *Huckleberry Finn*, which she hadn't started to read, for English; took her lipstick out of the pocket of her book bag; and went into the girls' room. It took a while to get the mascara off her cheek and more time to get her lipstick exactly right, so by the time she walked into Ms. Lustig's math class, it was after nine.

"Amanda?" Ms. Lustig said.

"I had a dentist's appointment," Amanda said, slipping into the desk next to Fern's.

"You have your homework?"

Amanda didn't answer.

"Everyone has handed the homework in."

"I'll give it to you after class," Amanda said.

She had recently noticed that adults, who used to treat her with great affection, even respect, no longer seemed to like her. Not the manager at Bread and Chocolate or the secretary in the office at Alice Deal, and certainly not Ms. Lustig. Not just today, either. She had felt it happening more and more in the last months, as if she had suddenly become unattractive to grownups.

"We're doing introductory geometry today," Ms. Lustig was saying. "Turn to page ninety-eight in your text."

Amanda had just opened her math book when a note from Fern was pushed across page ninety-eight.

So what happened? I thought you were supposed to meet Slade at Bread and Chocolate this morning.

Amanda slipped the note under her math book, wrote beneath Fern's words, and passed it back to Fern while Ms. Lustig was writing on the blackboard.

I don't know what happened.
I waited and he didn't come.

"Amanda, I wonder if you'd come to the board and do this problem from last night's homework," Ms. Lustig was saying.

Amanda folded her hands on her math book and pulled her shoulders up, looking past Ms. Lustig at the blackboard.

"I didn't do last night's homework," she said.

There was a shiver of giggles around her.

"Any particular reason for that?" Ms. Lustig asked in a starchy voice.

Amanda thought for a moment of what to say, but since she was only recently accustomed to lying, she was sometimes slow at it. She just said, "No, no reason."

"Hand it in tomorrow," Ms. Lustig said. "I'll make a note in my grade-book that it was late."

The note from Fern came back:

You're bold, taking on Lustig
like that. Sorry about Slade.
I saw him earlier on the back
field with a skinny blond
girl. Maybe he forgot.

Amanda's stomach fell at the news of the skinny blond, but she took the note from Fern and wrote back:

Maybe. No big deal.

Amanda went to the school nurse's office right after math class, skipping English, feeling as if she were about to die of some mysterious illness. The school nurse could find nothing the matter.

"No temperature. No swollen glands. No red throat. No headache—nothing I can see could be the matter except a rapid pulse." The nurse motioned her out of the room.

"But I feel terrible," Amanda said, sitting on the edge of the cot next to the nurse's desk, breathless.

"Go to class, and come back if you're not better by lunchtime," the nurse said.

Amanda started out of the room, moving slowly, hoping to avoid as much of English as she possibly could. She stopped by the girls' room, checked her hair, rubbed her cheeks pink, and then went down the corridor.

Fern had slipped a note into her locker.

I saw Slade in the hall after math class and asked him did he meet you at Bread and Chocolate and he said he forgot. I thought you'd want to know.

Fern

When Amanda looked up from reading the note, Slade

was on the other side of the hall, leaning against a locker opposite hers, his hands thrust in the pockets of his jeans, his head cocked, his cigarettes sticking out of his shirt pocket.

"I missed you at Bread and Chocolate," he said.

"I assumed you forgot." She pulled down her skirt, which felt too tight and was riding up on her hips.

"Something came up at home, so I left too late to stop for breakfast," Slade said. "Maybe we can hang out after school sometime."

"Wednesdays, I have…" She was going to say piano lessons, which was true, but piano did not seem to be the kind of instrument Slade would like, so she said guitar lessons.

"Guitar," he said. "Do you sing?"

He moved over next to her and leaned against the wall.

Amanda suddenly felt enormous. Her face was flushed, and she was sure her heart was pounding loud enough for him to hear.

"I sing a little," she said.

"Try me," he said.

"I mean, I can't sing now."

"Embarrassed?" He was smiling at her.

"I guess I am."

"So then I'll see you next week. Bread and Chocolate at

eight Tuesday morning," he said, brushing her shoulder with his arm. "Don't let me down."

Amanda was sitting in Spanish class, at the back of the room, her stomach wild with flapping butterflies. Ten minutes before the bell for eighth period, and she couldn't concentrate. When her name was called over the loudspeaker, she was thinking about what she would wear on Tuesday. Maybe she could persuade her mother to buy her a short black skirt that didn't ride up her thighs as high as the one she was wearing did.

"Amanda Bates," the voice blasted. "Please come to the office to meet your mother."

"Thanks a lot," Amanda said from the backseat of the van, her mother driving, Georgianna sleeping in the car seat next to her. "Now *everyone* at Alice Deal Junior High knows my mother was here."

"People have mothers," Mrs. Bates said. "It's not the worst thing in the world."

"That depends on your point of view," Amanda said, crouching down so her head was almost below the tinted window, in case anyone like Slade should look in.

Her mother was wearing a navy blue suit with a long skirt and white blouse, and she looked much older than she had looked even last week, Amanda thought, her hair laced with gray and a little scraggly.

"How come you wear those clothes?" Amanda asked. "You're only forty-two. A lot of the mothers I know wear blue jeans and short skirts and sort of young clothes."

"If the year continues with you the way it's going, darling, I'm probably going to be a hundred by summer vacation," her mother said.

"I guess you liked me better when I was smart," Amanda said.

"You're still smart," her mother said. "I miss your sweetness."

"Well, it's over, gone for good, so don't waste your time," Amanda said. "And don't tell me I'm just going through a phase. The way I am is permanent."

At the dentist's office, she asked her mother to wait in the van. "It won't take long," Amanda said.

"Don't worry," her mother said, opening her briefcase. "I've got plenty of work to do while I wait."

It was, Amanda realized, the first time she had gone to the dentist's without her mother trailing after her, and she felt a sudden surge of air beneath her feet as she pushed the "Up" button on the elevator.

CHAPTER FIVE

When Amanda got home from the dentist's, with no cavities but the promise of braces, she listened to a message from Fern on the answering machine.

"Call back immediately," Fern said. "It's sort of an emergency."

"Who's Fern?" Amanda's mother asked.

"Sort of my new best friend," Amanda said.

"I didn't know you had a new best friend," Mrs. Bates said, cutting up a banana for Georgianna and putting out cat food for Plutarch. "You should ask her over so we can get to know her. Maybe for dinner or a sleepover."

Amanda shrugged. She could hardly imagine Fern at her house for a sleepover.

"I doubt she'll want to come," she said.

"What's she like?" Mrs. Bates asked, slicing tomatoes for salad, then mashing the potatoes.

"I don't really know," Amanda said. Which was the truth. She knew very little about Fern.

"What kind of an emergency could it be?" her mother asked.

Amanda shrugged. "Who knows?"

She went upstairs and called on the telephone in her parents' room, lying on the floor with her head under the bed on the side where her mother slept, so Joshua, in his bedroom, couldn't hear what she said.

Fern had news about Slade.

"So I'm walking out of school today, thinking what I'm going to tell my mother about an F on my English test, and there's Slade with the skinny blond."

"Again?" Amanda whispered.

"But wait," Fern said. "I walk by him, not bothering to speak, and he calls, 'Fern, wait up.' So I do, and he says he has something important to talk to me about, so I follow him just far enough away so the girl can't hear us. And he says, 'So,' cocking his head like he does, clicking his lighter on and off, on and off: 'Tell me about Amanda.'"

"He said that."

"Exactly."

"Amazing."

"That's what I thought," Fern said. "I mean, you're only

in seventh grade, and he's in ninth. Not bad for a beginner."

There was a sudden silence on the wire, and then Fern snapped, "Gotta go. My mother's home from work in her usual lousy mood. I'll call you back."

Amanda could hear the voices, one high-pitched, probably Fern, the other lower, gravelly, saying distinctly just before the phone was replaced on the receiver, "Pack your bag. You're going to your father's."

When Fern called the second time, she was at her father's.

"It's a joke," she said. "When my parents got a divorce because they hate each other, my father moved two houses down the street—to make it easier for me to go back and forth, he said—but it's a nightmare. They see each other even when they carry out the trash, and don't speak."

"So is your father nicer?"

"Than my mother?" Fern laughed. "Who knows? He's brain-dead. He sits in the kitchen zapping his plastic-covered frozen dinner in the microwave and reading law briefs." She lowered her voice. "So I'm calling about the Club."

"What about it?" Amanda asked, her voice thin with worry.

"Your name came up after school today," Fern said.

"It did? How come?" Amanda asked.

"We're thinking you might like to sit at our lunch table tomorrow."

Amanda's heart flip-flopped.

"We always sit at the first table on the left when you come in the cafeteria."

"I know," Amanda said. Of course she knew. She checked that table every noon.

"You just have a way about you that we like."

"That's really great," Amanda said. "I like the Club a lot."

"We have rules," Fern was saying. "You know that."

"I've heard." Amanda was sitting in the kitchen now and had to be careful of what she said because her father was in the study watching the news and her mother was sitting at the dining room table helping Joshua with his homework.

"There's a dress code," Fern said. "Hair dye. Makeup. That kind of thing. And you choose a new name."

Amanda considered saying that she had already thought of the name Cheetah on the off chance that she was going to be invited to join the Club.

"I had trouble deciding between Fern and Hibiscus."

"I like Fern."

"It's okay." There was an odd catch in Fern's voice. "And we do things together. In fact, we do everything together."

"That's fine," Amanda said. "I mean, if you decide to ask me, I'm sure it'll be fine to do everything together."

"The important thing is that the Club comes first, before anything and anybody. Including your family," Fern was saying. "All for one, and one for all. That's the motto."

"I understand," Amanda said, giddy with excitement.

"Come to lunch tomorrow, and we'll see what happens."

When Fern hung up, Amanda was exhilarated. She didn't even hear her mother come into the kitchen and sit down next to her.

"You seem distracted," Mrs. Bates said. "Are you unhappy?"

Amanda shrugged. She didn't want her mother to see her exhilaration.

"Who's happy?" Amanda asked. "No one I know, except Georgianna, who doesn't know the difference."

"What are you, then?" her mother asked.

"Nervous," Amanda said.

For a fleeting moment, she wanted to tell her mother everything, the way she used to. That she was excited but also confused and worried, and heartsick for the simple, uncomplicated life she used to have.

But she certainly wasn't unhappy, and besides, in her new life as Cheetah, she didn't want her mother to know anything at all.

CHAPTER SIX

Slade was waiting in front of Bread and Chocolate when Amanda arrived on Tuesday morning, wearing the new black skirt her mother had reluctantly bought her at the Gap over the weekend and a gray cotton sweater, loose over the hips so she felt as if she looked thin. Slade didn't seem to notice how she looked, except to say she had lipstick on her teeth and did she want him to rub it off?

"No," she said quickly, almost dying of embarrassment, and rubbed the lipstick off herself.

He lit a cigarette, took a few drags, and then crushed it under his heel.

"Want something to eat?" he asked, motioning toward the coffee shop.

"I don't think so," Amanda said, sure she would be sick

if she swallowed anything at all. "I mean, maybe you do."

They went inside, and Slade ordered eggs and bacon and two blueberry muffins, a side of fries, and coffee, eating quickly, checking his watch.

"I'm starving, but I can't be late to school," he said. "I'm over the limit."

"Me too. I mean, I've been late twice so far since Thanksgiving," she said, shaking her head no when he offered her a bite of his muffin.

"They keep a close watch on me," he said.

"Because of your reputation, I guess," Amanda said.

"What do you know about my reputation?" he asked.

"Just that you're considered sort of wild."

"Did you hear that from Fern?"

"No, she didn't say anything. It's just that people around school have said you're not afraid of trouble and pretty much do what you want."

Slade was thoughtful.

"Kids admire you," Amanda added quickly. "I mean, they think you're sort of independent."

"I've had a reputation for trouble at Alice Deal, but it's not entirely true," he said, getting up and paying the bill. Amanda followed. "And it's not exactly a good thing. What about you? You're sort of mysterious to me. I can't place you in a group here."

"I don't know about me," Amanda said. "I used to be different in elementary school. More regular than I am now."

"Do you work?" he asked her as they left the coffee shop.

"What do you mean? At school?"

"You know. A job. I have a volunteer job after school at a pediatric clinic."

"Me too. I mean, not at a pediatric clinic, of course," she said. "I work at a shop in my neighborhood." She didn't know why she felt it necessary to say she had a job, which she didn't, but that was how it was with lying. "Lie a little," her father had often said to her, "and you'll find you have to lie a lot."

"I hear you may be asked to join the Club," Slade was saying.

"That's what Fern said," Amanda said.

"And you'll say yes?"

It seemed like a trick question, as if there were a right answer, which Amanda didn't know, but she said yes, she probably would join if they asked her. "Don't you like the Club?" Amanda asked.

Slade put his hands in his pockets and walked silently along beside Amanda, looking at her from time to time, making her blush.

"You're different than the rest of the girls in the Club," Slade said.

"Different how?" Amanda asked.

"How well do you know Fern?" he asked.

Amanda shrugged. "Not too well," she said. "I mean, she called me last night, but I've never gone over to her house or spent much time with her. Why?"

"I don't know why. I just can't see you in the Club, doing the stuff they do," he said.

"What stuff?"

"Ask Fern. It's her club."

"I haven't entirely made up my mind anyway, even if they do ask me," Amanda said, walking beside Slade up Nebraska Avenue. When they reached Alice Deal, Slade checked his watch.

"We've got ten minutes before the bell," he said. "I meet a couple of friends around the back of the building for a smoke before school."

He gave her a gentle punch in the arm. "Watch out," he said.

Amanda wanted to ask him why she should watch out, but he was gone at a clip around the building and she was left alone by the front steps as the students gathered in their tight groups, waiting for the beginning of school.

▲　○　■

There was a note from Fern on her locker.

Meet me in homeroom before class.
I want to know everything he said.
Did he try to kiss you?
Knowing Slade, he probably did.
                                    Fern

Amanda crumpled the note and put it in her book bag. She wasn't ready to talk to Fern. She didn't want to tell her everything. She especially didn't want her to know that Slade hadn't tried to kiss her, that he hadn't even tried to hold her hand. She was a failure at boyfriends, and she certainly didn't want Fern to know that. So she went into a stall in the girls' room, sat on the seat, put her feet up on the door so no one could see that she was there, and waited for the bell for homeroom.

Almost immediately, the door to the girls' room opened and she heard Fern's voice.

"Amanda?"

And then she could see Fern bending over and checking under the doors of all the cubicles. So Amanda put her feet down, unlocked the door, and walked out.

"Didn't you get my note?"

"I got your note," Amanda said.

"So?" Fern asked.

"Nothing happened."

"I don't believe you," Fern said. "Tell me the truth. You need to know there are no secrets if you belong to the Club."

"I'm not keeping any secrets," Amanda said. "I met him at Bread and Chocolate. He had breakfast. He smoked a cigarette, and we talked a little but not a lot, nothing personal—I mean, nothing really personal."

"Bummer. I expected something else."

Amanda shrugged. "Whatever."

"Slade has something in mind for you," Fern said. "I know him."

Later, in math, Amanda could see Fern was writing notes. She couldn't concentrate on what Ms. Lustig was saying; she was too agitated to think. It was beginning to look as if she finally had a group to join and a boyfriend as well. She could hardly contain her excitement.

When the bell rang, Fern passed her a note.

Don't forget. You're having lunch with us. And think about a new name in case we decide Yes.

At lunch, the members of the Club had saved a place for Amanda. She got yogurt and a salad in the cafeteria line and sat down between Fern and Anastasia.

"Don't ever eat cafeteria food," Fern said. "You'll be poisoned."

"That's what happened to Bronco," Anastasia said. "We bring our own lunch."

The Club sat in a corner of the lunchroom. With their black clothing, bold makeup, and dyed hair, they were immediately identifiable to anyone entering the crowded cafeteria.

"We're glad to have you at our lunch table,"Anastasia said. She was a tall, pale, white-powdered girl who spoke with an accent even though she was American.

There was a murmur of agreement around the table.

"We started to notice you after Halloween," Bronco said. "You kind of changed from when you first came to Alice Deal."

"You used to be nerdy," Fern laughed. "All those colored turtlenecks you wore."

Amanda had forgotten the turtlenecks, which she had worn in the sixth grade and at the beginning of seventh—bright blue and orange and yellow turtlenecks with jeans.

"We like people who are smart without being teacher's pets." A girl called Glo sitting at the end of the table was speaking.

"Smart and willing to break a few rules," Bronco added.

They all laughed.

"So how is Slade?" Anastasia asked.

Amanda noticed that Anastasia was wearing blue eye shadow striped across her eyelids and had a little black dot just above the side of her mouth.

"We hear you met him for breakfast."

"I did," Amanda said playing with her yogurt, beginning to feel as if she'd never eat again.

"Fern said he's your boyfriend," Bronco said.

"On the way to being her boyfriend is what I said, Bronco," Fern said. "Get it straight."

"He certainly is the most handsome boy in all of Alice Deal," Anastasia said.

"He's very nice," Amanda said.

"Nice?" Fern laughed, and ripples of laughter spread down the table.

"Not exactly nice, Amanda," Bronco said.

"Many things, but not nice," Anastasia said. She looked quizzically at her friends lined up along the lunch table. "Hasn't anyone told Amanda about Slade?"

"I know a lot about him already," Amanda said defensively.

"Then you know about the Home?" Glo asked.

"The Home?" Amanda asked, a sudden sinking in her stomach. "I don't even know what it is."

"Slade lives in a home for boys in trouble with the law," Fern said.

"I didn't know that," Amanda said thinly, the breath gone out of her.

"Well, now you do," Glo said.

"So you've got quite a boyfriend, Amanda," Fern said.

"He's not my boyfriend," Amanda said, gathering her tray and getting up from the table as the bell rang.

"Not yet," Fern said. "But almost."

Amanda walked home alone. Fern had waited for her on the lawn of Alice Deal, waving as Amanda came out the front door.

"We're voting this afternoon," she said.

"Good. I'm so glad." Amanda didn't know what to say, but "Good" seemed to be the right thing. Better than "Thank you, thank you, thank you," which is what she felt like saying.

But walking along Wisconsin Avenue, the traffic whizzing by, she was worried. Maybe they hadn't liked her after all. Maybe the only reason they were interested in asking her to join was because of Slade. Maybe, in the end, they'd vote No.

CHAPTER SEVEN

"Do you know anything about a Home for boys in trouble?" Amanda asked her father at the dinner table, hoping her voice sounded casual.

Mr. Bates shook his head. "I don't think I do," he said, reaching over to take away a spoon that Georgianna was banging on the tray of her high chair.

"It's someplace in Washington."

"Why are you asking?"

"I just wondered, that's why."

"Have you met any boys from there?" her father asked, his dark eyebrows raised in disapproval.

"I haven't," Amanda said, "but a girl at school told me some of the boys at Alice Deal live there because they've been in trouble."

"Do you know about this?" Mr. Bates asked Mrs. Bates, who was feeding Georgianna.

"I've heard about one," Mrs. Bates said. "It's called the Episcopal Home, and boys in minor trouble with the law live there under supervision."

Mr. Bates looked across the table at Amanda.

"Don't even ask me," Amanda said, sensing her father's next question. "I don't know any boys. I don't have a boyfriend. I hardly even have any friends."

"I thought you were beginning to make new friends," her mother said. "Like Fern."

"Fern?" her father asked. "I don't think I've met Fern."

Joshua gave his sister a conspiratorial look. "All Amanda did was ask a question, and you're giving her the third degree," he said. "You never did that when I flunked third grade."

"You're right, darling. We never did," Mrs. Bates said, getting up from the table with Georgianna. "But we got used to Amanda one way, and now she's changing."

"I've already changed," Amanda said.

After Mrs. Bates had carried Georgianna upstairs to bed and Joshua had gone up to do his homework, Amanda and her father cleared the table.

"I have to do my homework now," she said.

"Do the dishes with me first," her father said.

"I will, but I don't want to talk," Amanda said, sensing

a conversation ready to burst out of him, probably about her report card.

"Okay," he said.

"I just want to have a private life." She put the dishes in the dishwasher. "Every time I ask a question, like I did about the Home, I don't want you to think it *means* something."

"I hear you." Her father had assumed his speech-giving position, leaning against the kitchen counter, his arms folded across his chest.

"But I do want to talk about your last report card. Your homeroom teacher called your mother today before you got home," Mr. Bates said.

"There are plenty of people in the seventh grade in more academic trouble than I am."

"But I'd like to know what you think is going on with *you*."

"I'm just not as smart as I used to be," Amanda said.

"You're *just* as smart as you used to be," her father said.

Amanda shrugged.

"Something else has changed," her father said. "It's not only your bad grades. You dress in black. You dye your hair. You don't want to talk to us, and sometimes you act like your mother makes you physically sick."

"I can't help it," Amanda said. "And besides, you said we weren't going to talk."

"We're going to talk about your unacceptable grades, Amanda," her father said. "I want to see improvement, and quickly."

Amanda closed the dishwasher and pressed Start.

"Please explain these grades. A person doesn't change completely in six months."

"I don't know what's going on with my grades," Amanda said, picking up her book bag. "I'll let you know when I find out."

And she walked out of the kitchen and up the steps, dropped her book bag with the next day's unfinished homework in the hall, went into her bedroom, and locked the door.

It was dark out, and she turned off her light, lay down on the bed, and closed her eyes.

When Joshua knocked at her bedroom door, she was thinking about Slade. She was imagining him at the Home, which she pictured as a cross between school and a prison. In her mind, he was sitting on the front steps of the place, smoking. He had asked Amanda to meet him there and told her they'd do something like go to the movies or get ice cream or go bowling. She saw herself walking up the steps of the Home. A guard stopped her and asked what right she had to be there, and she said she was Slade's girlfriend and he had invited her and that was that. She lowered her eyes, pushed out her chin, swung her arms high and walked right past the policeman up the steps, and sat down beside Slade.

"Hi, sweetheart," Slade was saying when Joshua knocked on the door.

"It's Joshua," he whispered. "Not Dad, so you don't need to worry."

Amanda got up, turned on the light, and unlocked the door.

"Hi," she said, letting Joshua in and closing the door behind him.

"I came to talk," Joshua said, flopping across the bed.

"Where's Dad?" Amanda asked.

"Downstairs on a business call."

"He wants to know why I've turned stupid."

"You're still smart," Joshua said, pulling the bill of his baseball cap down over his eyes. "Andrew saw you with a guy at Bread and Chocolate this morning on his way to school. He says the guy's tough-looking with long hair and was smoking a cigarette."

"That would be Slade."

"And he lives at the place we were talking about called the Home?"

Amanda sat on the bed next to Joshua and drew her knees up under her chin. "I didn't say that," she said.

"You didn't have to," Joshua said. "I guessed."

Amanda shrugged. "Fern told me he lives in the Home for boys in trouble with the law."

"Wow. I wonder what he did."

"I don't know," Amanda said. "Anyway, don't tell."

"I'm not that stupid."

"I mean, don't even tell your friends."

"I won't tell Mom and Dad or my friends or anybody. But you've got to admit, that's sort of weird, Amanda."

"What's weird about it?"

"We don't know anybody with a criminal record."

"I suppose not." Amanda shrugged. "But every girl at Alice Deal wants to be Slade's girlfriend, so I'm not completely crazy."

"Is that why you dress the way you do?"

"Have you ever been to Alice Deal?"

"Never."

"Well, lots of girls dress like me, unless they're nerds. So it's normal. I look totally normal."

"And all the seventh graders have boyfriends?"

"Unless they're complete losers." She leaned back against the wall. "You should remember how it feels to be a loser."

"I do remember," Joshua said.

"Well, I'm finally maybe going to be asked to join a group."

"The Club?"

"They invited me to lunch today."

"And so you're really happy, right?"

"I think," Amanda said. "I'm not absolutely sure."

"Don't worry," Joshua said. "As soon as they ask, you'll be happy. I promise."

Long after Joshua had gone to bed and the lights were out in the house on Lowell Street, Amanda still couldn't get to sleep. She read for a while, and then she went downstairs to get a glass of milk. She turned on the television in the den and watched the report of a four-car accident in Silver Spring and a shooting downtown. When she climbed back under her covers, she tossed and turned, putting a pillow over her head to keep the light from the street out of her eyes. She was beginning to feel a sense of panic, a kind of breathlessness, an actual fear that she might be going crazy. She turned on the light and tried to read some more. But her hands were ice-cold, and she was beginning to shiver.

Finally, Amanda got out of bed and tiptoed down the hall to her parents' room. The door was open. Her father was sleeping on his side, snoring, as he often did. Her mother was lying on her back. Amanda couldn't tell if she was sleeping.

"Mom," she whispered across the dark room.

She stood quietly, waiting to see if her mother heard her before she called again. The second time, her mother stirred.

"Amanda?" She sat up in bed. "What's the matter?"

"I can't sleep."

Her mother crept out of her side of the queen-size bed, following Amanda down the hall to her bedroom.

"I haven't been able to sleep all night," Amanda said, climbing under the covers.

Mrs. Bates sat down on the bed beside her. "It's three o'clock in the morning."

"I know," Amanda said.

"You must be worrying about things, Amanda."

"Have you ever felt like you simply *snapped* and were about to stop breathing or go crazy?" Amanda asked.

Her mother crossed her legs. The light from the street glowed through the curtains.

"When I was in seventh grade at Marquette Junior High School, I had a yellow crewneck sweater," she began. "I wore it to school every day, convinced that if I didn't have it on, no one at Marquette would know who I was." She laughed. "That was pretty crazy."

"I guess," Amanda said glumly.

"Thirteen is hard," her mother said.

"I know."

"I remember feeling that nobody understood me."

"I don't even understand myself," Amanda said, but the edge of panic, a sense that she could simply die for no reason, was diminishing.

"That means you're normal, darling," her mother said, turning out the light, walking through Amanda's room on slippered feet, and going down the hallway to her own room.

And sometime, maybe immediately, maybe later—she didn't remember in the morning—Amanda finally fell asleep.

CHAPTER EIGHT

The next morning when Amanda, exhausted from lack of sleep, left her house, she saw Fern leaning against the Bates's front gate, a black hat pulled low over her forehead as if she were a spy.

For a single moment before her heart filled with the excitement of friendship, Amanda's stomach felt queasy and she wanted to go back into the house and climb into bed or go straight to Mirch Elementary, where she'd left behind her old, predictable life.

"Surprise," Fern said, looking Amanda over head to toe. "I thought we could walk together."

"Great," Amanda said, pulling up the hood of her ski jacket.

"Is that the only coat you've got?"

"I have an old coat of my mother's I wear for stuff like Christmas," Amanda said.

"Black?"

Amanda nodded.

"Today's all-black, and ski jackets are out."

Amanda went back into the house through the front door, hoping to avoid her mother, who was cleaning up the kitchen and talking to Joshua. She tossed her ski jacket on the floor of the hall closet, took out her mother's old black coat, which belted at the waist and had a high collar, and on second thought also grabbed a black beret from the shelf and stuffed it in her backpack, just in case everyone in the Club was wearing a hat today.

When she turned around to leave, her mother was standing at the landing with Georgie.

"I forgot something," Amanda said quickly.

Her mother didn't mention the coat, for which she was grateful.

"Is that Fern outside?" Mrs. Bates asked.

"We're walking to school together," Amanda said. "I don't have time to introduce you now."

"Of course," Mrs. Bates said. "I'm just very happy to see you with a new friend."

"Me too," Amanda said, closing the front door behind her and walking down the path to the gate.

"So you're probably wondering about the vote yesterday," Fern said.

"I guess," Amanda said, not wanting to appear too anxious. No wonder she hadn't been able to sleep.

"Well, we voted, and it was almost unanimous."

"What does that mean?" Amanda asked.

"It means two people need to get to know you better. They didn't vote Yes or No. They abstained."

"Which ones?" Amanda asked.

Fern shook her head. "I can't tell you that," she said, watching Amanda out of the corner of her eye as if she were assessing her face, her hair, the way she was dressed. "I brought a black skirt from home for you," Fern said, pulling it out of her book bag. "It's crushed velvet."

"I love it," Amanda said, holding up the skirt. "I've never had a velvet skirt."

"I used to wear it when I was fatter," Fern said, walking along, swinging her arms.

"I know I've gotten fat," Amanda said quickly, hurt by Fern's remark. "I used to be really skinny."

"You're not fat at all," Fern said. "The girls in the Club were just saying yesterday that they think you're really cute."

"Thanks," Amanda said, but she was uncertain whether Fern was telling the truth about her fatness.

As they walked down Connecticut Avenue together, Fern had a comment to make about everyone they passed.

"Anorexic," Fern said as they passed Alicia Holt, another seventh grader. "I happen to know she throws up in the girls' room if she eats anything at all."

"Belinda the slut," she said when a tall, slender redhead passed. "She's one of Slade's old girlfriends."

"He has a lot of them," Amanda said.

"Trillions," Fern said solemnly.

They walked up Nebraska Avenue toward Wisconsin Avenue.

"Do you know that guy?" Fern asked as they walked past a small, bone-thin seventh grader with his hair slicked back.

"I've seen him. He's in my English section."

"Billy Thorngill. Creep." Fern imitated the startled expression on his face. "Look at the way he dresses. He might as well be a girl."

Billy the creep, who was dressed in jeans and an olive drab jacket and a baseball cap, didn't look much like a girl to Amanda, but she didn't say so to Fern.

The rest of the way, Fern asked Amanda questions about her personal life. By the time they got to school, Fern knew everything about Amanda's life, even about Joshua flunking the third grade and Bruce's graduation present of CK1, and Amanda knew nothing about Fern except that she had a great interest in Amanda's relationship with Slade.

"Slade's had tragedy in his family," Fern said, assuming an appropriately tragic expression.

"Like what?" Amanda asked.

Fern shook her head. "It's sort of a private tragedy," she said earnestly. "He swore me to secrecy."

Amanda adjusted her book bag and folded her arms across her chest, feeling uncomfortable. There were beginning to be a lot of secrets between Fern and Slade, at least according to Fern.

"We're meeting Anastasia at Bread and Chocolate," Fern was saying, checking the clock across the street and turning into the restaurant. "She'll be here any minute."

They sat down at a table.

"I didn't tell any of the others. Only Bronco. But we have a surprise," Fern said, taking off her coat. "Do you drink coffee?"

"Sometimes," Amanda said. Which wasn't exactly true. She never drank coffee. It always seemed too bitter.

When the waitress came, Fern ordered two coffees and a Danish in a French accent.

"Do we have time before school starts?" Amanda asked. It was almost eight o'clock.

"Plenty of time. That's my surprise." Fern opened her book bag and took out three envelopes. She handed one to Amanda. "This one's yours."

Written on the front of the envelope, in large, sprawling handwriting, was their homeroom teacher's name. Inside was a note, which Amanda took out and read.

> *Dear Ms. Constantine,*
> *Amanda was ill last night so*
> *we took her to the doctor's*
> *this morning. She is feeling*
> *much better now. Please excuse*
> *her lateness.*
>   *Sincerely,*
>   *Mr. Bates*

"I used your father's name because Ms. Constantine probably doesn't know his handwriting," Fern explained.

"That's true. My mother always writes the notes," Amanda said, feeling ill even before she drank any coffee.

Fern pushed the other envelopes over for Amanda to read the notes inside. The first was from Fern's mother saying that Fern's grandmother was visiting only for one day and Fern had stayed home to be with her. The second was from Anastasia's mother, stating that Anastasia had an appointment with the foot doctor.

"Is there really something the matter with her foot?" Amanda asked.

"Oh no, of course not," Fern said, giggling and putting the notes back in her book bag. "But Ms. Constantine doesn't know that."

Amanda picked at the Danish, watching Fern rearrange her hat so it came down low on her forehead.

"Does this mean we're not going to school at all?" she asked.

"Later," Fern said calmly. "After third period."

"You've done this before?"

"Skipped school?" Fern rolled her eyes. "A trillion times. I've skipped school, been late for school, left school early." She folded her hands on the table, admiring her blue-black nail polish. "I do what I like," she said. "Everyone in the Club does."

"And you don't get in trouble?"

"Who cares? They're afraid of us," Fern said. "They only like little things they can control. Believe me. As soon as they can't control everything you do, they wish you were dead." She raised her hands in despair. "Even your parents. *Especially* your parents."

Amanda rested her chin in her hands, looking across the room into the middle distance. What Fern said was true, she thought sadly. Her parents had liked her better when she was good. When they knew what to expect from Amanda, when every day was just like every other and they heard no bad news from school. Now Amanda didn't even know what to expect from herself.

"I don't think my parents are afraid of me," she said quietly.

"Don't worry," Fern said with a sly smile. "They will be."

Amanda looked up and saw Anastasia running into Bread and Chocolate in tight black pants, a black V-neck sweater, and a beret. She pulled off the beret to show she had dyed her hair with a green stripe across the top.

"Like it?" Anastasia asked, sitting down.

"Very neat," Fern said.

"I like it," Amanda said.

"You should do it, Amanda," Anastasia said. "You have perfect hair for maybe a red stripe—like blood red." She took a sip of Amanda's coffee and ate the rest of her Danish. "So are we ready to go?"

"Where are we going?" Amanda asked.

"We're going to the Home, where Slade lives," Fern said. "I knew you'd want to see his house."

"We're going there now?"

"Exactly," Fern said. "Don't worry about school. You'll have to get used to the fact that people in authority who think they have control of our lives happen to be our enemies."

The Home was located off Nebraska Avenue in Rock Creek Park about two miles from Alice Deal. They took the M4 bus to the end of Nebraska and then walked the rest of the way.

"Cigarette?" Fern asked, taking a pack from her book bag.

"I don't smoke," Amanda said, quickly searching her mind for a reason to justify her answer.

Fern gave her an odd look.

"You told me you did," Fern said. "In the girls' room when I asked you for a cigarette, you said you didn't have one right now."

Amanda wrapped her arms around herself. "I just don't smoke in the morning," she said.

"All of the members of the Club smoke," Fern said coolly, a note of criticism in her voice, passing the pack of cigarettes to Amanda.

"You don't have to inhale," Anastasia said.

"Of course she'll inhale," Fern said. "What's the point if she doesn't?"

Amanda took a cigarette and put it in her mouth, and Fern struck a match.

"Breathe in," Fern said with irritation. "It won't light if you don't breathe in."

Amanda held the cigarette between her lips, breathed in when Fern put the match to the end of it, and choked.

"You must not smoke very much," Fern laughed. "But you'll get used to it."

Since there was no sidewalk, they walked along the road, Amanda pretending to inhale, taking the cigarette in and out of her mouth. Bare winter trees lined the road, and the rush-hour traffic on its way downtown flew past them.

"We're going to be killed by these cars," Anastasia said, moving behind Amanda so they could walk single file.

Eventually, they came to a small road with a sign at the end of it: THE EPISCOPAL HOME FOR BOYS. It was an old sign, bent backward so the only letters that a person traveling along the road could see were the O and M of HOME. Just beyond that sign was a second, smaller sign. NO TRESPASSING. Fern turned down the road.

"What about 'No trespassing'?" Amanda asked, trying to sound casual although she was beginning to suspect the worst.

"What *about* 'No trespassing'?" Fern asked.

"I just wondered what happens if you trespass," Amanda said.

"Nothing, as long as you act as if you own the place."

The road was long, lined with trees, the air damp, smelling of something like old mushrooms. There were no sounds along the road, not even birds or the brushing of branches. No voices at all.

"I wonder where everybody is?" Fern asked, pushing back the overgrown branches along the narrow road.

"At school," Anastasia said. "Where they're supposed to be."

"Usually there's a guard near the street," Fern said as the road suddenly opened and the dense line of trees ended. In the center of a large, unkempt field, a sorry-looking brick house with a large porch and pillars stood in ghostly silence. There were no cars in the circular drive, no signs of life, and behind the shuttered windows, the rooms were dark.

"No one's there," Anastasia said.

"Someone's got to be there," Fern said. "Someone's always there."

"You've been here before?" Amanda asked, rushing to keep abreast.

"Lots," Fern said, leveling her eyes at **Amanda**. "I know Slade *extremely* well."

"Right," Amanda said, uncomfortable. "I forgot."

Something in the way Fern spoke threatened Amanda, as if a whole story that included her was in the process of unfolding and she was the only one who didn't know the plot. Fern could be a danger to her, Amanda suddenly thought. She would have to pay attention.

The house was like a tomb—there were no sounds, no sense of life behind the front door. It was the kind of absolute silence that sends shivers up a person's spine. Even Fern hesitated.

"So tell me, what exactly is going to happen?" Amanda asked.

"I'm going to show you Slade's room. That's all," Fern said. "I'm sure you want to see it."

Fern pushed the doorbell. They could hear it ring on the other side of the door. She pushed and pushed the bell. Finally the door opened slowly to a tall, terribly thin man with a crisp, pointed beard.

A shaft of light fell across the threshold, and Amanda could see into the house. It didn't seem like a home for boys—more like a place where older people lived. The furniture was dumpy and dark, the rugs faded Orientals, the gloomy paintings on the wall in wide gold frames. It seemed too clean and too ancient to be a place where teenage boys lived.

"Hello, Fern," the man said. "I suppose you're cutting classes again."

"Dentist's appointment," Fern said coyly. "And my cousin Amanda is here from Philadelphia."

"Slade is at school," the man said, beginning to shut the door.

"Well, tell him I stopped by to show Amanda where he lived," Fern said. "I was hoping I could show her his room."

"Of course you can't see his room," he said.

"Well, I think I left my dangly earrings there. Sterling silver, from my grandmother." Fern looked as if she might make a dash past the man, but he blocked her way.

"As I've told you, I don't want you to come during the week anymore. Only on Sunday afternoons."

"Right," Fern said softly.

"The next time I'll call your parents." The man shut the front door.

"Jerk. He doesn't even know who my parents are," Fern said, running down the path toward the road.

"So you must go there a lot," Amanda said.

"Pretty often," Fern said.

"Tell Amanda about Slade and the Home," Anastasia said, slinging her arm around Amanda's shoulder.

"He got into trouble when he was twelve. He was in the sixth grade at Lafayette, and I was in fourth."

"He stole a car," Anastasia said.

"How could he steal a car at twelve?" Amanda asked, her stomach fluttering. It was one thing to know that Slade lived in a Home for boys in trouble and quite another to know *why*.

"Actually, a friend stole the car and he was along for a ride when they were caught," Fern corrected Anastasia.

"He went into a kind of prison, didn't he, Fern?"

"Not exactly. But he went to a place where he couldn't leave the grounds."

"What did his parents do?" asked Amanda.

"Parents!" Fern laughed.

"His parents are hopeless," Anastasia said.

"His mother left when he was little, and his father is always too busy."

"Where did she go?" Amanda asked, a little breathless, feeling out of her depth.

Fern shrugged. "Bolted with another man."

They climbed on the bus to Wisconsin Avenue.

"The Home is a kind of halfway house," Fern said. "Slade has to do community service and he has a curfew at night, but otherwise he's pretty free to come and go."

"So you guys have always been really close friends?" Amanda asked.

"More or less," Fern said.

Amanda took a seat behind Fern and Anastasia. Rush hour was over, the bus nearly empty, and listening to the dull roar of the bus engine, she thought about Slade at twelve years old, stealing a car. She had never known anyone who stole. She had never thought of doing it herself, not even of taking a dollar from the top of her father's dresser when the huge wad of dollar bills sat next to the loose change at night. Kids who stole were from a place in the city she had never been. And there was Slade. Just the picture of him, younger than she was now, stealing a car gave her a strange feeling in the pit of her stomach. She would ask him about it the next time she saw him, or maybe he would tell her on his own.

The bell was ringing for the first lunch seating when Fern, Amanda, and Anastasia arrived at Alice Deal and walked through the main doors and past the principal's office to their lockers.

"Just drop the note I wrote for you on Ms. Constantine's desk," Fern said. "She's probably in the teachers' lounge, so you won't even have to see her."

"But if I do?"

"Act like nothing's happened."

"I'll try," Amanda said, walking down the hall to her empty homeroom, putting the note on Ms. Constantine's desk, and then hurrying to her locker to change for gym.

Amanda was playing volleyball when the principal came to the gymnasium and asked to speak to her in his office.

"Change from your gym clothes, and I'll meet you there in a few minutes," Mr. Speth said.

"Why do you think he picked me?" Amanda stopped to ask Fern, who was sitting on the sidelines.

Fern shrugged. "Just don't say anything about what happened today. Tell him you weren't feeling well and you have a note to prove it."

"What if he calls my father?" Amanda asked.

"He won't," Fern said. "He's a wimp."

Mr. Speth sat behind his desk, his hands folded in front of him, peering like an owl over the rims of his half-glasses at Amanda.

"I've called you in about your grades."

Amanda's heart leapt up.

"I didn't know why you wanted to see me," she said. "I'm glad it's just my grades," she added without thinking.

He raised his eyebrows. "Is there more than your grades to worry about?"

"Oh no, it's just my grades," she said, breathless with worry. "But I thought I could have done something accidentally and not even known about it."

"We all worry about that," Mr. Speth said kindly. "I called Mirch this morning," he went on. "Your reports from last year are splendid. This year, by comparison, they are quite weak."

"I know."

"What's happened to you?"

"I don't know," Amanda said nervously. "I guess I'm just not as smart as I was in elementary school."

"Smart is smart, Amanda. It must be something else."

"Maybe," Amanda said, so relieved to be talking to Mr.

Speth about her bad grades instead of her bad behavior that she couldn't keep a half smile from her face.

"Things happen in seventh grade, especially with girls," Mr. Speth said. "A big new school and so many changes. Maybe you're even a little angry at your parents and your teachers."

"I'll work harder," Amanda said quickly.

"Good," Mr. Speth said. "We're expecting more from you."

Amanda stood up to leave.

"I hope you have some good friends in seventh grade, Amanda."

"I do. A few," she said.

"I'm glad. We all need friends, especially in the seventh grade," Mr. Speth said.

When Amanda came out of the principal's office, Slade was leaning against her locker.

"Hi," he said.

"Hi." She opened her locker to get her books.

"What's up in the principal's office? Trouble?"

He cocked his head in that way he had, and Amanda noticed for the first time that his eyes were olive-colored, wide-set, and warm. She liked his face.

"A little trouble," she said.

"Good." Slade gave her ponytail a pull. "I was afraid you might be too good for me."

She lowered her eyes, assuming what she hoped was a seductive expression, a look she had learned from love scenes on television and practiced in the mirror.

"I'm not *so* good," she said.

"I'm beginning to sense that," he said. "I understand you went to my house."

"Who told you?"

"Fern." He took a cigarette from his pocket and rolled it between his hands. "I didn't know you had it in you to skip school."

"It wasn't exactly my idea to go to your house, but I've skipped school plenty of times before," she lied.

"The place is pretty creepy, isn't it?"

"It really is," Amanda said.

"What did you do there?"

"Nothing really. Fern pretended I was her cousin visiting from Philadelphia. We kind of looked in the door and left."

"Fern's trouble." Slade swung his backpack onto his shoulder.

"She likes you, doesn't she? Sort of like a boyfriend."

"Who knows?" Slade replied.

Amanda took her books out of her locker and closed it, zipping up her book bag.

"What are you doing after school?" Slade asked. "I need to talk to you about something."

"I have to make up math homework for Lustig."

"Can you meet me on Thirty-eighth Street about three-thirty?"

"I may be late. I'm way behind in math," Amanda said.

"I'll wait. But don't let Fern know what you're doing."

"How come?" Amanda asked.

"Why do you think?" he asked, walking down the hall with her toward the auditorium for assembly.

"I don't know."

"She's jealous of you is why," Slade said.

CHAPTER NINE

Fern waited just outside homeroom while Amanda finished her math homework for Ms. Lustig.

"I thought you were meeting Slade after school," Fern said, falling into step with Amanda when she came out.

"I was." Amanda felt weak. Fern couldn't possibly have known she was meeting Slade. Unless, had he told her?

"That's weird." Fern took two cigarettes out of her pocket and offered one to Amanda, who took it and rolled it between her fingers.

"What's weird?"

Fern shrugged. "I guess he changed his mind again." She shook her head. "Slade's always changing his mind. It drives me crazy."

"What did he change his mind about?" Amanda asked, confused.

"I think I saw the skinny blond leave with him just a few minutes ago," Fern said casually.

So he had promised her one thing and done another, Amanda thought. In spite of herself, tears were gathering in her eyes.

"Where are you headed?" Fern asked. "Let's get out of here."

"I'm going home, but we can't go to my house," Amanda said. She couldn't imagine Fern with her cigarette and mascara and blue eye shadow sitting at the kitchen table with her mother.

Fern smiled. "I certainly don't want to go to your house. I dislike spending time with families—my own and everybody else's."

"I mean, I promised my mother I'd baby-sit my sister," Amanda lied.

"Fine by me. I'm just killing time until I meet Bronco at CVS drugstore after her shrink appointment."

They walked along Nebraska, Amanda thinking of Slade, maybe waiting for her on Thirty-eighth Street, leaning against a lamppost smoking, maybe with the skinny blond. How was she to know? Who could she believe?

It was getting dark and colder. The air had a feel of snow coming. It was too late to figure a way to catch up with

Slade or to get rid of Fern. Besides, Amanda thought, if he'd gone off with someone else, he probably didn't want to see her anyway.

"Bronco's meeting me here at five," Fern was saying. "She wants to redo her hair tonight." She started through the automatic doors of CVS, and Amanda followed half-heartedly, feeling low, wanting to go home.

"Stick close," Fern said. "I'll show you something you'll need to know if we decide to ask you to join the Club."

"Okay."

"Just follow me while we walk around the aisles. I'll start in Hair, and we'll talk like we're really fascinated with what the other is saying."

"Sure," Amanda said, her heart feeling hard against her chest.

"Whatever you see, don't react."

"Got it," Amanda said. It seemed like the right thing to say.

Fern slid her backpack off one shoulder and unzipped it at the bottom, stopping in Hair Products and taking a box of Beautiful Hair in a pale yellow package off a shelf. The color was Magenta.

"I think this will be perfect with Bronco's complexion, don't you?" Fern asked, looking up and down the empty aisle.

"Really perfect," Amanda said, short of breath, now knowing exactly what Fern had in mind but unable to believe she was actually standing beside her.

"I think if she sort of dyed one side Magenta and the other Sunflower, she'd have a really original look." Fern spoke in animated stage whispers, and Amanda hardly caught the movement out of the side of her eye when Fern slipped the package of Beautiful Hair in her backpack. Fern moved on down the aisle to the barrettes and hairpins and scrunchies, taking one with navy blue and white stripes off the rack and holding it next to Amanda's Sable-colored hair.

"Wrong for you," she said. "But you do need something cool for your ponytail." She unzipped Amanda's backpack and swiftly dropped the scrunchie in the place where Amanda kept her pencils and pens.

"There," she said. "Now you have something for your ponytail."

Amanda stood by the barrettes, her heart pounding, a criminal, carrying a stolen scrunchie in her book bag. Certainly she would be caught as she left the store. The alarms would sound as she passed under the sensors. The police would appear, put her in handcuffs, and call her parents.

"Follow me," Fern whispered.

In the makeup aisle, Fern opened tubes of lipstick and

checked the color. "I like really dark. Almost muddy." She puckered her thin, maroon-outlined lips. "Like this." She showed Amanda a tube of Dark Chocolate.

"I love it," Amanda said, feeling sick, as she watched Fern drop the tube of Dark Chocolate into the pocket of her black coat.

Fern checked her watch. "Bronco should be here any minute," she said. "She sees the shrink for depression. She's on medication."

"No kidding," Amanda said.

"She's had a terrible life. I'll let her tell you about it."

Fern moved to the teen magazines, where she opened one and looked at the table of contents.

"I hate this magazine," she said, putting it back. "It's totally stupid."

Amanda followed Fern to the front of the store, her mind a whirl, trying to think of a way to get out of CVS before they were caught, as they surely would be. Taken to the Second Precinct. Her father would be called straight from his office to come to get her.

When Bronco walked down Aisle Three, where the film was, Fern had just put a box of Kodacolor 400 in the pocket of her black coat.

"A successful afternoon at CVS?" Bronco asked.

"Magenta," Fern said. "Perfect with your eyes."

"So we're done." Bronco slipped her arm through Fern's, and Amanda followed them to the door.

No one had noticed. Amanda checked the dark-haired young woman at the cash register. She showed no interest in their departure. The sensors at the door failed to sound an alarm, and they were out on Connecticut Avenue, walking in the stripes of streetlights.

"I've gotta go now," Amanda said, heading up Newark Street. "It's really late."

"I hope you had a good time at CVS," Fern said.

"Was that your first shoplifting opportunity?" Bronco asked.

"My first," Amanda said. She wanted to say, *I didn't do it. I was there, but I did nothing. Zero. A passerby. Not even a friend of the criminal.*

"Well, get used to it," Bronco said, smiling. "It's the way we keep up with the latest fashions."

And laughing, their arms around each other's shoulders, Fern and Bronco headed in the direction of school.

Amanda turned toward home. She felt as if she had fallen into a hole and through the earth to the other side of the world. Nothing made sense to her. As she headed up Newark Street, she wondered if she would ever be able to steal. So much had changed in her life, and in ways that surprised her. Six months ago she could not have imagined being the girl she was this afternoon, standing in CVS, her hair dyed, her skirt alarmingly short, wearing makeup, an accomplice to shoplifting. Something about Fern was too powerful for friendship. Maybe the only interest Fern had in Amanda had to do with Slade.

She wanted to get home and climb into bed and sleep until Christmas break. They'd go to Pennsylvania as they always did right after Christmas, the whole family piled in the car, heading north on the turnpike to Grave's Ski Lodge, where the snow was usually thin, grass peeking through the white patches, the ground wet beneath their skis. But at night the family sat around a big fire in the lodge and drank hot chocolate, shoulder-to-shoulder. For a moment, she couldn't wait.

Which was what she was thinking when Slade came up behind her as she turned onto Lowell Street.

"Hi," he said.

"How did you get here?" Amanda asked.

"Walked. I thought I'd come to your house and see if you were here," he said. "I waited on Thirty-eighth Street like I said I would, and you never came."

"Fern was waiting for me outside homeroom," Amanda said. "She said she'd seen you with someone else."

"Who?"

"A skinny blond."

"A skinny blond?" Slade's forehead crinkled. "I don't know who she's talking about."

"That's how she described her."

"Well, she was wrong," Slade said.

"She even knew I was meeting you on Thirty-eighth Street."

Slade shook his head but didn't say anything. Amanda thought for a moment, wondering how Fern could have known if Slade hadn't told her. "How did she know?" Amanda asked.

"She may have guessed. She knows we're getting to be friends," Slade said. "But I certainly didn't tell her."

At the corner of Lowell and Thirty-fourth, Amanda could see the bright lights of the kitchen of her yellow house.

"That's where I live," she said. She was thinking of what to say to him. Whether she should bring up the shoplifting. She had thought of Slade as the kind of boy who would admire breaking the law. Perhaps he would be pleased to know she had a blue-and-white scrunchie stolen from CVS in her backpack. But she wasn't sure about Slade yet. She wasn't even sure about herself any longer.

"Nice," Slade said, standing on the sidewalk surveying the Bates's house.

"There're zillions of more-expensive houses. This one is just ordinary," Amanda said.

"It looks friendly."

"I like that too," Amanda said, thinking quickly about what she was going to do with Slade. Probably her mother was in the kitchen, cooking and playing with Georgianna. Certainly Joshua was home by now, sitting at the dining room table struggling with his homework. Amanda thought that Slade did not exactly have the look of a boy her mother would be glad to meet.

"Are you rich?" he asked.

"No way," Amanda laughed.

"But you have things like bikes and cars and stuff," Slade said, leaning against a tree, still looking at the Bates's house.

"Not a lot of things. One television. Just regular things that everybody has."

"Which room is yours?" Slade was looking up.

"It faces the back," Amanda said, feeling a sudden thrill at his interest in her room, seeing a picture projected on the screen of her mind: Slade sprawled on her bed, leaning against the headboard while she sat at the end of the bed, her legs folded under her.

"That room is my parents' room," she was saying, pointing at a window. "That's the bathroom, and that's my brother Joshua's room. My sister Georgianna's and mine are both on the back."

"So each of you has your own room," Slade said.

"Don't you have your own room at the Home?"

"I've never had my own room. Not even when I lived with my father. We had a one-bedroom apartment with a den, and I slept in the den," Slade said. "At the Home, I have two roommates."

"Did you know them before you moved into the Home?"

"I've had about six roommates since I moved there. All strangers. Guys are always moving in and out." Slade started up the walk. "Can we go in?"

"You mean you actually want to go into my house?"

"That's what I mean," Slade laughed. "Through the front door and into your house."

Amanda could imagine her father's face when he came home from work and saw Slade in the kitchen, hanging over the center counter smoking a cigarette, in his baggy jeans and T-shirt, his hair long and curly.

Hello, her father would say. *Who's your friend, Amanda?*

Hey, Slade would say. *My name's Slade.*

Slade? her father would ask.

Slade. That's it. My full and complete name. He'd sit down at the kitchen table and grind his cigarette out with the sole of his shoe.

So you're a friend of Amanda's, her father would say.

Boyfriend, to be exact, Slade would reply.

Boyfriend. You live nearby?

I live off Nebraska Avenue, at the Home.

The Home? her father would say. He had a way of repeating everything a person said, which drove her crazy.

You know, the Home, Amanda would say. *We talked about it last night at dinner. Mom told you about it.*

Of course, the Home for boys in trouble with the law, Mr. Bates would say. *I certainly remember that conversation.*

You got it, Mr. Bates—what's your first name?

John, Amanda's dad would say.

You got it, John, Slade would say. *I'm one of those boys with a police record.*

Amanda started across the street toward her house, checking her watch. An hour before her father came home. "I guess you can come in," she said. Her mind was blank with worry. What would she say to her mother? *This is my boyfriend, Slade?* Or, *This is my friend Slade from the Home. You remember the Home?* And what in the world would her mother think of Slade, with the pack of cigarettes peeking over the top of his pocket, his long hair, and his leather jacket?

"Are you worried about introducing me?" Slade asked. His tone was inquisitive, not combative. "I'll bag the cigarettes."

"Don't worry," Amanda said, quickly walking up the path. "I was just a little freaked because my parents are strict. I've never brought a boy home, so I don't want them to think I have a boyfriend."

"You don't have a boyfriend," Slade said, following Amanda onto the front porch.

When she opened the front door, she could smell cookies in the oven and hear the sounds of the washing machine, the radio in the background, and Georgie babbling in her high chair.

"Mom," she called from the hallway, putting down her book bag and hanging her jacket on a hook. "I've brought a friend home."

CHAPTER TEN

Amanda sat in the window seat in the kitchen after Slade left, light from the streetlight streaming through the window, Plutarch lying across her lap, purring.

He had stayed only for a minute, long enough to meet her mother and stuff his pockets with warm chocolate chip cookies.

"I was just walking Amanda home," he said. "And now I've got to go home myself."

"You live nearby?" Mrs. Bates asked.

"Off Nebraska Avenue," Slade said. "A place called the Episcopal Home."

"Oh yes," Mrs. Bates said, lifting Georgianna out of her chair. "I know of the Home."

"Bye-bye," Georgianna said, waving to Slade.

"Goodbye," Mrs. Bates said. "I'm glad you came over."

"So am I. You have a beautiful house." He shook her hand and walked out the back door.

Now Amanda was trying to answer her mother's questions while her mind was a hurricane of desperate thoughts about Slade and stealing and Fern and the Club and the skinny blond who might or might not have been real.

"So, darling," Mrs. Bates was saying. "Do you happen to know why Slade lives at the Home?" She tried to sound casual, as though she were making conversation and had no interest in Slade's living arrangements at all, but Amanda knew better.

"I don't know," Amanda replied. "His mother left when he was small."

"He doesn't have a father?"

"He has a father, but his father doesn't want him very much, I guess."

"That's terrible," Mrs. Bates said. "No wonder he's been in trouble."

Amanda shrugged. "I have no reason to think he's been in trouble," she lied deliberately, not wishing to start a conversation that could go badly. "He's never told me."

"What *has* he told you?" her mother asked, turning the answering machine on so they wouldn't be interrupted by the telephone.

"Practically nothing," Amanda said.

"Well, I thought he was very polite."

"He's not my boyfriend, if that's what you were thinking."

"I wasn't thinking that at all," Mrs. Bates said. "I was thinking he's your friend and how nice it is to have a friend who's a boy."

Amanda lifted Plutarch off her lap and put him on the floor.

"But I hope you don't think he's a criminal because he lives in the Home," she said.

"I'm sure he's not a criminal," her mother said.

"And I hope you won't call the Home to check into his background," Amanda said. "Like sometimes you get too nosy."

At first her mother didn't answer, but as Amanda was leaving the kitchen to go upstairs, she said, "You'll have to trust me. You used to."

"What choice do I have?" Amanda asked. She wanted to talk to Joshua, but first she needed to be alone in her own room, to put the scramble of the day on shelves in her mind, to organize her thoughts so she could know what to do, as she used to. But then, after lying on her bed staring at the ceiling for a while, she felt like talking to someone. So she came out of her room and peeked into Joshua's.

Joshua was trying on his soccer uniform, standing by the

full-length mirror in his bedroom and arranging the knee pads.

"I'm playing goalie in winter soccer. First string for Montgomery County," he said.

"That's great, Joshua." Amanda flopped down on his bed.

"It's my favorite position, because I'm a pretty good catcher and an amazingly shifty runner," he said, examining himself in the mirror, an expression of deep seriousness on his face.

Amanda actually wanted to have a conversation with Joshua. She wished he were older, old enough for a girlfriend, old enough to keep company with petty criminals like Fern, no longer interested in playing goalie for Montgomery County, old enough to understand what was going on with her as her mother did not.

"Did you see Slade come into the house?" she began.

"I saw him, but I had to try on my new uniform, so I didn't come down to meet him," Joshua said. "Is he your boyfriend?"

"I don't have a boyfriend," Amanda said.

"Is he the same person Andrew saw you with at Bread and Chocolate?" Joshua asked.

"He *is* the same person, but he's not my boyfriend."

"He looks sort of tough."

"He sort of is and sort of isn't," Amanda said, turning over onto her stomach and watching Joshua look at himself in the mirror. "He came over here to see our house because he's never known anyone who's rich and lives in a big house."

"We're not rich," Joshua said. "We're regular."

"Compared to him we are. He's extremely poor." Amanda gave her brother a narrow-eyed look, the kind that used to wither him when he was small. "He probably doesn't even have enough to eat, and his mother's bolted. He pretty much has to fend for himself."

"So how do you know him?" Joshua asked, practicing his throw in front of the mirror.

"He goes to Alice Deal. He's a friend of Fern's."

"Fern from the Club?"

"She's sort of head of the Club."

"Are you a member yet?"

"They've half asked me."

"Well, today when I talked to Andrew, he said his sister turned into a nightmare when she went to Alice Deal, smoking cigarettes and skipping school and kissing every boy in junior high, even the nerds."

"Don't be like Mom and Dad. I have enough problems with the two of them," Amanda said, getting up from the bed.

"I just hope you don't join up with a bad group of friends. That's all I hope," Joshua said. "You might turn into someone I'd never want to know."

"I've already turned into someone you'd never want to know," Amanda said, looking at her reflection in the full-length mirror.

Fern called just before dinner. She had more news.

"So I was talking to the skinny blond," she said. "You know the one I mean, Slade's kind-of girlfriend, the one who's sort of your competition."

"I don't know her," Amanda said. "There're hundreds of skinny blonds at Alice Deal."

"Well, this one's in ninth grade. I never noticed her before," Fern was saying. "She wears these tiny flowered skirts and she has legs like a giraffe's. She's drop-dead gorgeous."

"I don't know her," Amanda said. She didn't mention that Slade had come over that afternoon and said he didn't know what skinny blond Fern was talking about.

"Well, she wouldn't be asked to join the Club, because she's just the wrong type, kind of the popular type instead, but she and I are becoming friends, and she told me that Slade got a girl pregnant and the baby is already born and has been adopted by people in Pennsylvania. That's what she heard from a girl who knew it from another friend who knows Slade from somewhere."

"I don't know what to say about that," Amanda said, feeling the now-familiar sinking in her stomach.

"Well, it sounds true to me. Just like Slade," Fern said.

"It's like a story from a trashy romance magazine."

"Right. Exactly. It's, like, just amazing. I never knew anybody my own age to have a baby," Fern said.

"I don't know if I believe it," Amanda said. "What's this blond girl's name?"

There was a moment's hesitation. "Melissa," Fern said. "So I hear from Bronco that Slade met up with you and went to your house."

Her voice sounded matter-of-fact, but Amanda knew she was being accusatory.

"He was just walking around and we ran into each other, and he stopped to see my mother and have cookies," Amanda said cautiously.

"How does your mother know him?"

"She doesn't *know* him. She'd never seen him until today."

"I thought he followed you home to get a look at your house," Fern said.

Amanda didn't reply. So someone was watching her. Maybe Bronco. Maybe others, a whole team from the

Club, keeping watch on everything she did, where she went, whether she talked to Slade in the corridors of Alice Deal, whether she had friends who were not members of the Club, whether she had other boyfriends. For a long time, all during the fall at Alice Deal, she had had the sense that she was invisible, that no one knew who she was or was interested in knowing her. Now, suddenly, she was smothered with attention.

"Amanda?" Fern asked. "Have you dropped the phone?"

"Slade's not my boyfriend, if that's what you're wondering," Amanda said. "He's probably the boyfriend of Melissa, like you said."

"I wouldn't worry about Melissa if I were you," Fern said. "She's sort of too proper."

"I'm not worried," Amanda said. "So I'll see you tomorrow before school?"

"That's what I was calling about. We're all meeting at seven-thirty in front of Alice Deal."

"I didn't think the Club had meetings."

"This isn't exactly a meeting," Fern said. "The members who don't know you want to meet you, and besides, something has come up."

"I'll be there," Amanda said.

"And don't say anything to your parents about going to

the Home today," Fern said. "Also, keep the shopping trip at CVS to yourself."

"I'm not crazy," Amanda said, hanging up the phone.

In the kitchen, her mother had just started to make vegetable lasagna, cutting up eggplant and zucchini. Amanda took the telephone book out of a drawer, looked up the Episcopal Home for Boys in the white pages, copied down the number, and went upstairs to her parents' bedroom.

"I'm calling for Slade," she said when a woman answered the phone. "This is Amanda Bates."

"He can't come to the phone," the woman said. "Does he have your number?"

Amanda gave it to her.

"Don't count on his calling back," the woman said. "We have study hall at night and an early curfew."

"I understand," Amanda said.

She replaced the receiver, went into her own room, and lay down on the bed, and by the time her mother called her for dinner, she had fallen into a deep, dreamless sleep.

CHAPTER ELEVEN

On the way to school, Amanda stopped at a CVS to buy Saffron hair dye. The store was a different CVS, the one closer to her house, on Lowell Street. Nevertheless, she had a moment of panic. Already the word could be out about her shoplifting and she would be recognized in the little cameras stuck around the ceiling recording the activities of shoppers. She could see herself elongated in the small, round mirror above Hair Products, and just seeing the tiny reflection of her body, she was thrilled and terrified because she had left CVS the day before with a stolen scrunchie, evading the cameras and mirrors.

She was lightheaded and couldn't concentrate. She felt as if she were on a roller coaster, thrown back in the seat and holding tight to the railing in front of her as the car flew up the tracks over the metal hill, leaving her stomach in the air above her head, and speeding down the other side of the hill.

When she got to Alice Deal, Bronco and Fern were sitting on the steps, and in the distance Amanda could see Anastasia and another member of the Club she hardly knew hurrying in their direction. Fern was smoking.

"My boyfriend's here from New York," Fern said when Amanda, Anastasia, and the other girl arrived. "He gave me this."

She stuck out her arm to show them a silver bracelet with FERN engraved on it in block letters.

"I thought you had a thing for Slade," the other Club member said. She turned to Amanda. "I'm Citronella." Then she sat down on the steps, took her makeup out of her book bag, and began to apply mascara without a mirror.

"Wrong number," Fern said. "Slade belongs to Amanda."

Anastasia sat down on the steps next to Citronella.

"After our conversation yesterday, I thought you might have dyed your hair last night," Anastasia said to Amanda.

Amanda took the box of Saffron dye from her book bag. "Tonight," she said.

"Cool," Citronella said. "A smashing color for you. Saffron. Maybe I'll change my name to Saffron."

"What's up, Fern?" Anastasia asked. "Did anybody get caught going to the Home yesterday?"

"Not a chance we'll be caught," Fern said.

"So what are we doing here in the middle of the night, when I should be sleeping?" Citronella asked.

"We're here about Amanda," Fern said.

"Great," Anastasia said. "Have you chosen a name, Amanda?"

Amanda wasn't ready. She felt her throat closing, her voice trapped in her windpipe, her heart out of control.

"So?" Fern asked.

"Cheetah," Amanda said as coolly as she could.

"Cheetah," they said in unison.

Fern narrowed her eyes. "Cheetah." She thought for a moment, repeating, "Cheetah," with a flourish. "Not bad."

"So we're here for Cheetah's initiation into the holy sanctuary of the Club," Citronella said.

"She was sort of initiated yesterday," Fern said.

"Yeah?" Bronco asked. "How?"

"At CVS," Fern said.

They all laughed.

"Good haul?" Citronella asked.

"Hair dye for Bronco, some film and lipstick for me," Fern said. "A medium haul. Not impressive, but Cheetah was fine. She didn't flinch."

"Good," Anastasia said. "But I bet you were nervous."

Amanda took a deep breath.

"Not really," she lied.

"She may not be the best at doing the job herself," Fern said, "but she's an okay sidekick."

"What do you think, Cheetah?" Citronella asked. "Would you agree with Fern's evaluation?"

"I don't know whether I could ever steal anything myself. I'd probably freeze."

"You'd be okay," Anastasia said.

"Fair," Fern said. "Not a lot of promise in shoplifting, but you have other advantages, Cheetah."

"Thanks," Amanda said, wondering what advantages she could possibly have for them.

"There're just a couple of things you ought to know about the Club." Fern opened her book bag and took out a couple of sheets of paper. "Here." She handed the two type-written pages of names to Amanda. "These are the girls that we ignore. We're not unkind to them. We simply pretend they aren't there. Dead. Invisible. They don't exist."

Amanda looked at the sheets of paper.

"There are a lot of names here," Amanda said.

"One hundred and ten so far," Fern said, putting on Citronella's lipstick.

"Why don't we like these girls?" Amanda asked.

"Various reasons," Fern said. "Mostly, we just have standards. You'll get used to them."

"You didn't know this about the Club, Cheetah?" Citronella asked.

"I didn't know about a list," Amanda said. "I mean, I never thought there would be a list of girls to ignore. It's a little weird."

"All groups are like this," Fern said.

"That's not exactly true, Fern," Anastasia said. "Groups are exclusive, but we're so organized."

"That's right," Fern said. "So this is a list of girls who will *never* be asked to join the Club."

"Do they want to join?" Amanda asked.

"I don't know. They haven't been asked," Fern said in exasperation.

"I don't understand," Amanda said.

"We have this list, right?" Fern said. "Every time we meet someone, we make a decision on them. No, Maybe, or Yes."

"That's what we did with you," Bronco said. "It wasn't No with you, but it wasn't Yes, either. It was Maybe. Wait and see."

"If it's No on someone, it's No forever," Citronella said. "That's the deal."

"You were a Maybe," Anastasia said. "That's what I mean by 'organized.'"

"Are you saying we can't have friends outside the Club?" Amanda asked.

"You can have boyfriends, of course."

"But no regular friends?" Amanda asked.

"It's not that you can't have regular friends outside of school," Anastasia said. "It's just that you can't have regular friends in school, unless they're members of the Club."

"That's kind of strange," Amanda said.

"It may be strange, but those are the rules," Bronco said.

"And we need to know by tomorrow if you're joining or not," Fern added coolly.

"If I don't join, does my name go on the list?" Amanda asked.

Fern ground her cigarette out on the cement.

"No one has ever turned the Club down," she said.

Inside Amanda's locker, there was a note from Slade, which he must have dropped through the narrow slit at the top that morning when he came to school.

> Dear Amanda,
> Trouble. See you at lunch.
> Slade

Her blood turned to ice water. She slipped the note into the pocket of her jacket, waved to Bronco standing by the water fountain, and sat in the back of the room for fourth-period history.

Slade was standing outside the principal's office after Amanda, sitting in the back of history class, was called over the loudspeaker to come there. The collar of his black leather jacket was turned up, and he wasn't smiling.

"I'll wait until you finish with Speth, and then I've got to talk to you," he said. "I'll be by your locker."

"You're not mad, are you?" Amanda asked.

But he had turned away and was walking down the hall, leaving Amanda to face the principal with her stomach turned upside down.

Mr. Speth was standing in front of his desk, leaning against it, his arms folded across his chest, his tie askew.

"Sit down," he said. He held out the note with her father's forged signature. "Did you write this?" he asked.

"No, I didn't," Amanda said, sitting on the couch beside his desk, her hands wet.

"Why don't you tell me what happened?"

She didn't want to cry, not here, but she was beginning to feel as if she wouldn't have control over it. She slid back on the couch.

"Start at the beginning," Mr. Speth said.

"Yesterday I met some friends, and we decided to skip school in the morning."

"Which friends?"

"I can't tell you. It wouldn't be fair."

"But one of them wrote the note."

"It doesn't matter," Amanda said. "I might as well have written the note myself because I handed it to Ms. Constantine with my father's made-up signature."

"I'm interested to know what you did," Mr. Speth said.

"We went to the Home."

"The Home?"

"Where Slade lives," she said.

"I see," Mr. Speth said. "But Slade was at school, so why did you want to go to his house in the middle of the day when he wasn't there?"

"I can't answer that," Amanda said.

"Your friends have a different story of what happened yesterday morning."

Amanda folded her hands. "The story I told you is the one I remember," she said, determined not to make things worse by implicating Fern and Anastasia. "I don't know everything about my friends."

Mr. Speth handed Amanda the note. "I'm planning to call your parents this afternoon to tell them what happened," he said. "And I'd like you to take this letter home and show it to your father.

Amanda stuffed the note in the pocket of her jacket.

"It was a surprising thing for you to do, Amanda," Mr. Speth said.

"I know," she said honestly. "I surprised myself."

"And that's all that happened yesterday?" he asked.

"Pretty much," Amanda said. She wanted to tell him about the shoplifting, which was heavy on her mind, but she didn't.

"See me first thing tomorrow after you've spoken to your father." Mr. Speth held open the door for Amanda to leave.

She stood and walked out of the principal's office, past the secretary, to her locker, where Slade had said he would be. Instead, Fern was standing there with Anastasia, but Amanda just headed to the library to work on her social studies project during free period. She could hardly breathe.

Fern followed her. "Cheetah," Fern said. "Wait up."

"I can't talk," Amanda said.

"We've got to talk," Fern said. "We need to coordinate about skipping school." It was too late to coordinate, and Amanda probably wouldn't have been able to lie outright to the principal, whatever Fern asked her to do.

"Later," Amanda said, and turned the corner into the

library, sitting down at the farthest table, her back to the door.

She hadn't even opened her notebook when Fern slipped into the chair next to her and whispered, "So what did you say to him?"

Amanda caught her breath. Her face was hot, her mouth was dry, and she felt as if she were going to have a heart attack.

"I didn't mention you or Anastasia," she said. "But I told the truth."

"What is the truth?" Fern asked, cocking her head.

"I told him what I had done. I didn't say you'd forged the note."

"Not bad," Fern said, a slow smile spreading across her face. "Not bad at all, Cheetah."

CHAPTER TWELVE

When Amanda got home, she could hear her mother in the kitchen, chattering to Georgianna. She waited for a moment to see if her mother had heard her, and then she tiptoed upstairs to her room. Plutarch was lying in a shaft of sunlight on her bed, and she closed the door, lay down on the bed, and burrowed her face in his soft yellow fur.

First Slade had not been waiting for her after her meeting with Mr. Speth. Then he had not been at lunch, and she hadn't seen him at the end of the school day, either.

"He disappears like that, and no one can find him," Fern had said when Amanda asked if she had seen Slade. "Maybe he's with one of the girls in his class, maybe he's skipping school. Why?"

"I just wondered," Amanda had said, unwilling to say too much.

"Just don't count on him and you'll be happy," Fern had said.

Now she lay on the bed, looking out the window at the disappearing sun and wondering what her father was going to say about the forged note, what she was going to tell him about shoplifting, what it was Slade had wanted to say to her. Her life was coming apart at the seams.

Joshua walked in without knocking.

"I heard you come upstairs," he said, lying at the foot of the bed. He looked as if he wanted to say something more but couldn't get it out.

"What else did you hear?" Amanda asked, sitting up and pulling Plutarch across her lap.

"Not much," Joshua said.

"You're lying."

"I heard Mom on the phone with Dad when I got home from school."

"And did you hear what she said?" Amanda asked. "Do you know what I did?"

"She said you skipped school," he said. "Is that true?"

"It's true," Amanda said. "It's even worse than that. Was Mom furious?"

Joshua shook his head. "Not furious," he said. "She was very quiet. She sat down at the table and put her chin in her hands and didn't talk at all."

"Great," Amanda said. "That's worse. I made her miserable."

"You always used to be so perfect," Joshua said. "I was the one who worried them."

Amanda crossed her legs, putting Plutarch in her lap.

"The Club invited me to join this morning," she said.

"So are you going to?"

"They have a list of all the girls who will never be asked to join the Club, and if you're a member, you have to ignore those girls and only be friends with members of the Club."

"It sounds terrible," Joshua said.

"I thought I liked those girls," Amanda said. "I really thought they were the ones I wanted to be friends with."

"So are you joining?"

Amanda shrugged.

"I hadn't decided this morning when they asked me. I mean, I was thinking about it, and then I was caught for skipping school today, and I told the principal what happened and the other girls didn't tell him."

"They lied?" Joshua asked.

"I don't know what they said."

"Which girls?"

"Fern. You don't know about the others. One is named Anastasia and the other's called Bronco."

"I thought Fern was your best friend."

"Me too," Amanda said.

"Weird. I don't know about junior high," Joshua said. "You're making flunking third grade seem like nothing."

After Joshua left, Amanda sat on her bed for a very long time, not thinking, just staring across the room at nothing in particular. The telephone rang several times. She could hear her mother in the kitchen preparing dinner, and the happy gurgling of Georgianna, and the pounding of the soccer ball Joshua was kicking against his closet door. She heard her father's car in the driveway, the car door opening and closing, the front door opening. She sat on her bed waiting for him to come upstairs.

"Amanda." Her father's voice had the familiar flatness it got when there was a problem.

She put Plutarch on the floor, stood up and brushed the cat hair off her black skirt, and pulled her hair back into a ponytail.

"Yes," she replied.

"May I come in?"

She could have said, *No, I'm extremely busy dyeing my*

hair the color of a purple grape. I'm putting on Plum blush and don't want to be disturbed. I'm leaning out the bedroom window smoking a cigarette and don't wish to talk.

"Yes," she said, opening the door.

He had changed clothes. Somehow, she was glad of that. He wasn't wearing his dreary gray business suit and tie, with his glasses flat against the bridge of his nose. He had changed into jeans and tennis shoes, his glasses were on the top of his head, and the expression on his face was not ice-cold, which it was when he was angry.

She reached into her pocket and took out the note Fern had written and forged his name on.

"I guess you want to see this note."

He took it and read it, then handed it back to Amanda.

"I'm sorry," she said. "It's probably illegal, right? Forgery. Maybe I could get sent to a juvenile detention home."

"I doubt that," her father said, sitting in the small rocker beside her dresser. "It's not the worst thing in the world. Many people have done the same thing, including my sister, Charlotte, when she was young. And they have grown up to be wonderful, successful, happy people without prison records."

"What did Aunt Charlotte do?" Amanda asked, wondering how she could tell her father that forging the note was only one of the things she had done.

"She skipped school, went to the movies with her friends, signed a note from our mother saying she was ill, and ended up in trouble. And now she's a doctor," Amanda's father said. "I'm not that worried about you, darling."

"I did worse than Aunt Charlotte," Amanda said quietly.

"Worse?"

"I did more than skip school," she said. She had not been planning to tell her father, but she couldn't help herself. She wanted him to know. She wanted to turn her drawer of bad secrets upside down so he could see them all.

"Do you want to tell me?" he asked in that way he had that meant *Tell me immediately*.

"Yesterday I went to CVS with Fern—the friend Mom mentioned—to get hair dye for another girl, named Bronco. And Fern shoplifted."

"Shoplifted?"

"Lipstick, hair dye, and film. She's almost professional."

"And what did you do?"

Amanda went over to her book bag and pulled out the blue-and-white scrunchie. "This," she said.

"You stole that?" her father asked, his voice chilly.

"I stood right beside her while she did, so I might as well have done it myself."

Her father was quiet. He leaned his head back, looking at the ceiling, then closed his eyes.

"That's true. You might as well have," he said.

"I'm sorry," she said softly.

"Where did you go yesterday besides CVS?"

"The Home," she said. "The place we talked about at dinner, where boys who have trouble with the law live."

"And do you know why you did all of this?"

Amanda didn't answer at first. She looked out the window at the bare dogwood tree in the garden and felt tears welling in her eyes. Why she did it made her sad even to say out loud.

"Sometime in the middle of the summer after sixth grade, I began to feel different. Just like a different person had turned up in my body, and I didn't know what to do with her," Amanda said. "I didn't know where she belonged."

"I understand, Amanda," Mr. Bates said sternly. "But it's not an excuse for following a group of people who break the law."

"I know. I really know."

"Thank you for telling the truth." Mr. Bates put his hand under Amanda's chin and tilted her face toward him. "There's still a little purple lipstick left over, and some mascara," he said.

When her father left, Amanda opened her closet door. She took off the short black skirt and loose sweater that concealed her hips; slipped on her blue jeans, a little tight in the seat since sixth grade, and one of her brother's T-shirts, and went downstairs.

"I have some news," her mother said as she walked into the kitchen.

Amanda leaned wearily against the kitchen door, expecting the news to be bad. "What?" she asked, an edge to her voice.

"We have a guest coming for dinner."

"I'm not up for guests," Amanda said. "I'll eat in my room."

"Slade called for you before you got home."

"He did?" Amanda asked, sinking into a wooden kitchen chair. "How come?"

"He didn't say, but I invited him for dinner," Mrs. Bates said. "I'm sorry not to have asked you first, but I didn't know you'd gotten home yet."

"Mom!" Amanda exclaimed.

"He was very nice on the telephone, so I said, 'Would you like to come for dinner?' and he said he'd love to. He'll be here at seven-thirty."

Amanda put her head in her hands.

"I can't believe it," she said, mortified at her mother's intrusion in her life. "You invited him to our house without asking me."

"He's your friend," her mother said.

"I wouldn't be so sure about that," Amanda said, leaving the kitchen. "And even if he is, this is the worst day in my whole life, and I'm going to bed right now forever."

CHAPTER THIRTEEN

Amanda was in her bedroom changing again when Slade arrived. She heard the front doorbell's ring, her mother's high-pitched voice, and her father's booming greeting, and her heart felt as if it had popped out of her chest and dropped onto the floor.

"You've got company," Joshua said, opening the door to her bedroom, where she stood in her underwear.

"Out of here," Amanda snapped.

"I'll tell him you'll be down in a couple of days."

She took her red skirt out of the closet and then tossed it on the floor without trying it on. She knew how it looked. Terrible. She was tired of the black skirt, and her jeans were too tight. For that matter, all of her pants were too tight, and she certainly couldn't wear makeup in front of her parents. She had absolutely nothing satisfactory to wear. She grabbed a shirt and ran into her parents' room, rifling through her mother's closet, but all of her mother's skirts looked as if they belonged to a middle-aged lawyer, which they did. Except for a very tight black satin skirt that Amanda was trying on when her mother walked into the room.

"I don't think so," Mrs. Bates said. "It's not exactly right for dinner at home with the family."

"I have *nothing* to wear."

"He's in jeans."

"I know exactly what he's in. Baggy jeans and a black leather jacket with the collar up," Amanda said while wiggling out of her mother's skirt, hoping not to rip it at the seams.

"Wear what you always wear."

"You mean now or last year?" Amanda was beginning to feel hysterical.

"Whatever you'd like, sweetheart, but you ought to come down soon."

Amanda ran down the hall to her room, pulled on the black skirt and loose black sweater she had been wearing, and brushed her hair quickly into a ponytail.

In the mirror, her face looked white without makeup, but she didn't dare put any on. Her father would ask her at dinner if she was dressed for a funeral. And her mother would say something embarrassing like *You have such lovely natural color, Amanda.* She put on dirty black tights and her clunky black shoes, and picked up a load of laundry to carry downstairs to the laundry room so Slade would think she was busy with domestic chores and not personal fashion.

He was sitting on the kitchen counter when she walked in, drinking a glass of iced tea and holding Georgianna, as if he'd been there a hundred times before.

"Hiya," Amanda said, flying through the kitchen and down the basement steps with her laundry. "I'll be right back."

She dumped her laundry in the washer, stalling for time to calm down. She poured in detergent, turned the washer to Normal, and walked slowly up the steps, taking deep breaths.

The dining room table was set for a party, with a table-cloth, which they never used on weekdays, and candles and even the best plates. Joshua raised his eyebrows when Amanda walked into the dining room, where he was finishing setting the table.

"It's not exactly what happens when Andrew comes over for dinner," he said.

"What do you think's gotten into Mom?" Amanda asked.

"Beats me," Joshua said. "It's like you're getting married."

"Shut up, Joshua," she said. "Like I told you, he's not even my boyfriend."

In the kitchen her parents were chatting with Slade, asking him about the Home, how he liked it and what it was like. Mrs. Bates dished out mashed potatoes and chicken onto a serving platter and said dinner was ready.

"Wow," Slade said, walking into the dining room, where candles were flickering and classical music was playing on the stereo. "This is amazing." He lifted Georgianna into her high chair. "Do you do this every night?"

"Sometimes," Mrs. Bates said. "If we're all here for dinner."

Amanda was glad for the candlelight. At least it concealed the bright pink of embarrassment on her face.

"So you were telling us about when you moved to the Home," Mr. Bates was said as they all sat down.

"Two years ago," Slade said, perfectly comfortable, as if it were the most normal thing in the world to discuss his criminal record with strangers. He looked up from his plate. "I suppose what you really want to know is why I'm there."

"I do," Joshua said.

"When I was twelve, an older guy I knew stole a car in southeast Washington, and I was with him. We decided to drive cross-country, but we got caught in Ohio."

"You knew how to drive?" Joshua wanted to know.

"He drove."

"Where was your family?" Mrs. Bates asked.

"My mother left when I was small, and my father had a new girlfriend and was busy with her."

"Well, that *is* very interesting," Mr. Bates said.

"What do you mean, 'interesting'?" Joshua asked.

Mr. Bates smiled pleasantly at him. "Interesting to learn how a boy..." He thought for a moment. "Qualifies for the Home."

After dinner, Amanda and Slade waited on the couch in the den for her father to finish a business call and take Slade home before his curfew.

"I'm really surprised you wanted to come to dinner," Amanda said.

"I didn't call to invite myself to dinner," Slade said. "I called to ask you about something Fern said, and then your mother just asked me to dinner."

"She told me. My mother's always taking over my life like she's in charge of it," Amanda said, awkward, adjusting her body against the back of the couch. "What did Fern say?"

"She said you'd been passing stories around about me with members of the Club," he said.

"Me?"

Slade shrugged. "That's what she said."

"What kind of stories?" Amanda asked, suddenly imagining Fern grabbing Slade's arm in the corridor at Alice Deal, whispering secrets to him.

"She said you told everyone in the Club terrible things about what I tried to do with you."

"You didn't try to do anything," Amanda said.

"I know that."

"And I didn't say anything to anyone. You probably don't believe me, but Fern was always suggesting that maybe you, you know, tried to kiss me or something, and I said no, never. We weren't boyfriend and girlfriend. You did absolutely nothing at all."

"I told you, Fern is trouble," Slade said. "She likes to control everyone, so she tells lies, and pretty soon kids hate each other and like Fern. I've known her a long time."

Amanda was quiet, remembering some of the things Fern had told her about Slade, wondering now if they were true or if Fern had made them up. Amanda was wondering whether she should ask Slade herself when Mr. Bates came into the den.

"Ready to go?" he asked Slade.

"If you decide to join the Club, you have to watch out for yourself," Slade said to Amanda as they followed Mr. Bates outside to the car. "It's not like other groups. It's more like a gang."

"I'm beginning to see that," Amanda said as Slade got in the passenger seat of her father's car.

"So I'll see you after school tomorrow?" Slade asked.

"Tomorrow?" She shook her head. "Tomorrow after school I have a piano lesson."

CHAPTER FOURTEEN

The next morning, Slade was waiting in front of Alice Deal, leaning against the steps, his hands in his pockets.

"You're late," he said when Amanda arrived, wearing the red skirt and white V-necked sweater she had gotten for her birthday. No makeup.

"I didn't know you'd be here," she said.

"You should have known." He smiled. "Here I am."

She was conscious of the way she was standing, one hip higher than the other, one shoulder down. She felt older than she had the day before.

"The Club was looking for you."

"Who in the Club? Fern?"

"Exactly. She was waiting here with Bronco and Citronella."

"I wonder how come?" Amanda asked, following Slade up the steps.

"They're expecting you to join the Club today," Slade said.

"I thought maybe they'd changed their minds since I told Mr. Speth about what happened with the forged note."

"But you didn't tell on them." Slade opened the large front door and pushed his pack of cigarettes deep into his pocket. "Fern liked that. You took the blame and protected your friends."

Amanda shrugged. "I don't know if they're really my friends," she said, imagining her days at Alice Deal without the Club and feeling lonely. "I think the only reason Fern wanted me to join the Club in the first place was because she likes you and she thought you liked me."

"She's right," Slade said, walking with Amanda to her locker. "I mean, I do like you. I even like your parents. I *never* like parents. I mean, the truth is, parents never like *me*, but your parents actually listened to what I was saying."

"I guess they did," Amanda said. "That's something I didn't realize before last night because they're my parents. You never notice the good things about your parents."

"They made me feel like a real person," Slade said.

Amanda leaned against the locker, holding her books in her arms.

"So?" she asked. "What's up?"

"I don't know," he said, giving her a gentle box on the chin. "What's up with you?"

Overnight, everything had changed for Amanda, as if a thunderstorm had come and cleared the air. When she looked at them through Slade's eyes, her parents were much better than she had thought. The Club, which only yesterday had been more important to her than anything, turned out to be not so important after all. And most confusing, bewildering since she had never even particularly liked boys, was that she wondered whether or not Slade was her boyfriend. It seemed normal to be with Slade, as if they were regular friends and had been all their lives, even though she'd known him for only a few days. Later, maybe this afternoon, she'd ask him. Something like *Are you my boyfriend?* or maybe *Am I your girlfriend?* She wanted to know the conditions of their friendship.

There was a folded-up note on the bottom of her locker, and she opened it.

> *Dear Cheetah,*
> *We've got to know TODAY if you're joining the Club. We only have one place left, and if you don't join there's another girl we're thinking of asking.*
> *Fern*

Amanda put the note in her pocket, lifted her book bag over her shoulder, and waved goodbye to Slade.

"Maybe I'll walk you to your piano lesson?" he called.

"Sure," she said.

Fern was sitting by the door when Amanda walked into Spanish class.

"Cheetah." Her voice was hoarse.

Amanda stopped.

"Did you get my note?"

"I did," Amanda said, her heart beating hard. "I just got it out of my locker."

"So?"

Amanda was still afraid of Fern, afraid of the power she had and the kinds of things she might say to some of the other girls. But Amanda had made her decision, and it surprised her—to think of the way she used to long for Fern to be her best friend knowing, as she now did, how different they were, how difficult their friendship would have been.

"I decided no," Amanda said.

"How come?" Fern demanded.

"It just feels like the wrong thing for me to belong to a club."

"Is it about the list?" Fern asked.

"I don't like the list," Amanda said, thinking for a

moment. "But that's not the only reason. I just don't think I'm a Club kind of person after all."

"So now that you have a boyfriend, why bother with a club, I guess," Fern said, an edge to her voice. "You better take advantage of the moment. You know Slade. He won't stick around for long."

Amanda shrugged. She wasn't going to respond to Fern's challenge this time.

Slade waited after school for Amanda and walked her home in the drizzling rain to her piano lesson.

"Are we boyfriend and girlfriend?" she asked him on the way down Wisconsin Avenue.

"What does that mean to you?" Slade asked.

"I don't know," Amanda said. "I've never had a boyfriend."

"It means trapped to me," Slade said.

"'Trapped'?" Amanda licked rainwater off her lips.

"A little like the Club. I'm not ready for a girlfriend with rules about what I can do and who I can talk to and this rule and that rule. When Brianna Baker was my girl-friend, I almost went crazy. She didn't want me to talk to any girl with blond curly hair. She didn't want me to hang out with my friends on the weekend, and she insisted that I call her every single night at nine o'clock."

"Boring," Amanda said.

"It *was* boring. Too many rules," Slade said, brushing the wet hair off Amanda's forehead.

Amanda walked along quietly beside him, thinking about friends, whether it was good enough to be Slade's friend and not his girlfriend. Whether he would stick around.

"What about Fern?" she asked.

"Fern was my friend when I was in trouble," Slade said. "Not anymore. You're a better friend for me."

"What kind of friend?" Amanda asked, wrapping her arms around herself.

"A best friend."

They had turned down Lowell Street, and the sky was darkening, the odd sound of winter thunder rumbling in the distance, the air thick.

She knew what she was going to ask him. She had been thinking about it, thinking about the best way to say it, but instead she blurted out, "Fern says you are the father of a baby."

It sounded formal the way she said it, young and a little odd.

"Fern is wrong," Slade said.

"Then why do you think she said that?"

"To cause trouble, the same reason she told me you were saying terrible things about me."

"You're telling the truth."

"I'm telling the truth. That's the one rule if we're going to be best friends," Slade said. "Tell the truth."

They had come to the front of Amanda's house. Her piano teacher's car was there already.

"I wish you could come in," Amanda said. "I'm sure there're cookies."

"I have to get home early," Slade said. "I just wanted to walk you home."

He smiled his wonderful crooked smile and waved goodbye.

When Amanda walked into the kitchen, Fern was on the phone.

"I wanted you to know," she said. Her voice had lost its strength. "Remember the skinny blond I mentioned to you, Slade's sort-of girlfriend?"

"Melissa."

"Right. Melissa," Fern said. "We've asked her to join the Club."

"That's great," Amanda said, her voice even. "I wanted to tell you something, too. Remember what you said about Slade and a baby? Well, I asked Slade, and it isn't true."

"Oh, that was just gossip," Fern said.

"You mean you knew all along it probably wasn't true?"

"I was pretty sure it wasn't," Fern said. "Girls can tell a lot of bad stories that aren't true."

"I guess they can," Amanda said.

After she hung up, she took a few cookies, poured a glass of milk, and opened the door to the garden, going out into an afternoon that had become sunny suddenly, as if someone had turned a spigot off and stopped the rain. The grass was wet, the December air had the smell of holiday excitement, the bare branches were dripping water like so many tiny fountains. She sat down on her old swing set, the wet swing a little creaky as she pushed gently back and forth.

In the kitchen, her mother was beginning to cook dinner, and Amanda could see Georgianna's head just above the windowsill. She had never known until this moment that she loved winter, the coming of Christmas, with ice skating and family dinners and evenings around the fire, nothing but long days with her best friend, starting her life over again as Amanda Bates.

SUSAN SHREVE is the author of several highly acclaimed novels for young adults and children, including three books about Amanda's younger brother—*The Flunking of Joshua T. Bates, Joshua T. Bates Takes Charge,* and *Joshua T. Bates in Trouble Again*—as well as *The Goalie,* which *Publishers Weekly* described in a starred review as "eloquently crafted in simple, direct prose . . . both hard-hitting and a joy to read."

Susan Shreve lives in Washington, D.C.